War at
Spanish Saddle

He was tall, sitting in the saddle with a forward slouch. His rangegarb was trail-stained and he wore a pair of Colt .45s, in holsters tied down with rawhide thongs – which meant he was fast. Mead Conant wore the guns as if they were part of his body and he had the gunfighter mark on him, easy, confident – but edgy.

They said he was no equal when it came to gunplay. Lots of people figured he would return to his own part of Arizona sooner or later and now he was there. But no longer was he the kid who had seen his home-steader father and brothers gunned down twelve years before. This was Conant of the big six-gun reputation, a man who had carried bitter hatred for Arch Tamblyn and his Flying Spur spread ever since that gun-filled night of his boyhood when they killed his kin and burned their homestead.

Conant vowed the killers would pay – and he always kept his promises!

War at Spanish Saddle

HUGH MARTIN

A Black Horse Western

ROBERT HALE · LONDON

© 1957, 2001 A.A. Glynn
First hardcover edition 2001
Originally published in paperback as
War at Spanish Saddle by A.A. Glynn

ISBN 0 7090 6933 2

Robert Hale Limited
Clerkenwell House
Clerkenwell Green
London EC1R 0HT

Typeset by
Derek Doyle & Associates, Liverpool.
Printed and bound in Great Britain by
Antony Rowe Limited, Wiltshire

One

News of Mead Conant's return reached Arch Tamblyn by way of Cliff Dignan.

Flying Spur business took Dignan, Tamblyn's middle-aged, rawhide tough foreman, into Tombstone, and he spotted Conant when his business was completed and he was stepping from the Oriental, wiping his mouth with the back of a mahogany-brown hand. He stood stock still, watching the raw-boned rider who came along Allen Street, sitting his saddle loosely.

It was Mead Conant all right. He was older, but it was Conant.

He was tall, despite the forward slouch of his body; he wore trail-stained range garb and a black sombrero from under which lank strands of tawny hair escaped, but it was the guns, holstered at his thighs, that claimed Dignan's attention. Big, bone-handled Peacemaker Colts. The worn holsters were tied down with rawhide thongs, which meant the wearer was fast. But Cliff Dignan needed no telling about Mead Conant's gunspeed. He'd been hearing stories from all points of the frontier during the last seven or eight years. They all said Conant was hell on wheels when it came to gunplay.

Lots of people figured Mead Conant would show up in his own part of Arizona sooner or later and, sure enough, here he was.

Cliff Dignan watched the slow-riding horseman progress along Allen Street. The eyes in Conant's craggy face were scrunched against the glare of the desert sun that punished Tombstone's weatherboard and adobe structures and touched a sparkle to the languid plumes of dust rising from under the hooves of his bronc. The Flying Spur foreman turned his face from the street as Conant came nearer. He propped his weight against one of the Oriental's ornate pillars and pulled his scuffed hat over his eyes as the gunfighter rode past. Then, he swivelled about and regarded the back of the tall, gun-hung rider.

He saw Conant hitch his bronc at the rack fronting a small eating house and watched him swing his long-legged length from the saddle and stride lithely into the restaurant.

With Conant out of sight, Dignan moved for his roan, tail-swatting flies at the Oriental hitch-rail, forked the animal and hit a smart clip out of Tombstone.

Mid-afternoon found him riding through Huajillo, the little cowtown nestling on the edge of the Spanish Saddle range. At six in the evening he was pouring out his story to Arch Tamblyn on the gallery of the Flying Spur ranch-house.

Tamblyn, paunchy and with a handlebar moustache

spiking from under a broken beak of a nose that was monument to some long-ago cow-crew brawl, sat in a tilted chair with his heels hitched on the gallery rail. A hard man was Arch Tamblyn, as hard a Confederate Army veteran who ever shucked out of Texas and into Arizona. He built the little empire that was the Flying Spur spread with blood, sweat and, maybe, a few tears. He brought his cattle-outfit into being by using some fair means – but many more foul ones.

His face was an impassive, wind-burned mask as he listened to Cliff Dignan's story. When the foreman concluded, the rancher jetted a stream of tobacco juice over the gallery rail.

'You sure it was young Conant?' he asked.

'No mistakin' him. You know that sameness the Conants have—'

'Had,' corrected Tamblyn.

Dignan swallowed.

'Yeah – had. It was Mead Conant, all right, I'd know him anywhere. He's older, of course, around twenty-eight, but it was Conant.'

'Does he look like he really has that reputation we keep hearin' of?'

'Yeah. He looks as mean as a tarantula an' he wears a pair of big Colts like they was part of his body. Walks like a gunslinger, too, easy an' confident, but sorta edgy at the same time.'

Arch Tamblyn spat again. Something that was almost a smile settled on his weather-punished features.

'Would you say Mead Conant is a sentimental man, Cliff?' he queried.

'Sentimental? With those big Peacemakers an' that reputation? I wouldn't gamble on Mead Conant havin' a lead peso's worth of sentiment in his whole carcass, Arch.'

'I would,' answered the rancher slowly. 'I'd gamble on him havin' enough sentiment to ride into this country by way of Moroni Creek, just to look at that burned-out old nesters' roost. I figure that's what Conant would do as soon as he reached these parts from Tombstone – if he was a sentimental man.'

'And?' asked Dignan.

Arch Tamblyn regarded his foreman with two glittering eyes that had lost nothing of their intensity although he was nearing seventy. He answered slowly and deliberately, as though giving Dignan round-up instructions.

'There's a wall of high rim-rock overlooking Moroni Creek, Cliff. A couple of good rifle hands, like you an' Spade Lacy, for instance, could find a position up there that would look plumb square down on the old homesteader's trail.'

Cliff Dignan understood and signified so by nudging his six-gun loose in its holster. It was purely a reflex action.

'If I was you, I'd look up Spade pronto, an' get over to Moroni Creek without wastin' any time,' Tamblyn instructed.

Dignan went.

Arch Tamblyn re-crossed his legs on the gallery rail.

'Mead Conant!' he growled in a scornful, low voice.

He spat over the rail.

*

Mead Conant put Tombstone behind him with a belly-full of mediocre cooking under his belt-buckle. He headed his bronc's nose for the Spanish Saddle range and rode steadily.

As he rode, he thought.

He thought of the tiny homesteaders' cabin down on Moroni Creek, remembering it as it had been that night twelve years before, when he was a sixteen-year-old kid. He remembered the bullet-slashed fury of that night when Flying Spur riders swooped out of the rim-rock. He remembered his father, slumped in death over the sill of the shattered window; his nineteen-year-old brother, Lloyd, shot through the head the moment he tried to take his father's place at the window, and his older brother, Clay, shoving him out of the rear door of the cabin and telling him to run for the brush and keep on running. He recalled how he reached the brush, threw himself down to catch his breath and saw Clay, a magnificent and hopeless figure in the light of the blazing cabin, crouching gunfighter fashion, slamming slugs at the raiders until they gunned him down.

The memories caused him to touch spurs to the bronc's hide and quicken the animal's pace.

When he reached the edge of the Spanish Sadd'e range, he purposely circled the town of Huajillo. To a large extent, it was Arch Tamblyn's town and he wanted to make his return to his boyhood surroundings as inconspicuous as he could.

Warm summer night had sifted down over the wide, desert-edge land when Mead Conant reached Moroni

Creek. In the half-hearted darkness, he found the old homestead trail, running alongside the creek. It was an ill-defined track now, for the years had all but obliterated it with scrub and thorn. Conant followed it until he reached the ruin of the cabin his father and brothers had built. The torches of Arch Tamblyn's gunnies had razed it, but nature had gentled the blackened ruins with high weeds.

Conant sat his mount before the ruin for a long time.

Here, was the spot where Clay made his last stand that fear-fraught, flame-lit night. Up the rise, at the back of the gutted shambles, was the clump of brush where he lay with a panting heart, watching his brother slug-pounded into the dust.

In the darkness, he quirked his lips into a smile that had no humour in it. Men in Dodge, Abilene and a dozen other cowtowns had seen that tiger's smile lift the corners of Mead Conant's mouth a split second before he went for those big, low-riding guns. Those who had merely been crippled by Conant's bullets could tell you the smile was a danger sign while those who had the fullest experience of the tall man's gunspeed were rotting in boot hill graves.

Conant urged the bronc along the hazy trail, heading for where it snaked around an outcrop of high rimrock. He rode slowly, still thinking.

He saw the muzzle-flash of a rifle lance out from half-way up the nearby rimrock and pitched himself to one side out of the saddle in that almost non-existent space of time between the flash and the hard bark of the rifle. He felt the hot breeze of the whining shell fan his face as he was in mid-air and he hit the shaly dirt while the flat clatter of the shot echoed over the wide land.

Conant rolled over to his back, drawing both Colts in the same action. He lay there, quite still and marking with his eye the spot on the dark face of the rim-rock rise from which the would-be bushwhacker had fired.

There was a brief silence, then a voice sounded from up the wall of rock:

'Y' hit him, Spade?'

Then an answer:

'Seems so, but the light was damn bad.'

And Mead Conant lay silent and waiting.

From off the rim-rock came the clatter of hooves. Conant saw two men, leading horses, silhouetted against the purple night-sky as they came down to the trail from the shadowed bulk of the high-rearing rimrock.

He waited, rolling slowly and soundlessly on to his stomach, watching the outlines of the men and their led horses coming along the trail towards him. So they were coming to investigate. That suited him fine.

The boots and hooves crunched nearer over the hard dry ground and Conant fired at the leading silhouette, not shooting to kill.

He heard a yelp of pain echoing on the heels of the clattering shot and he started rolling over and over, so that he was no longer in the position marked by his shot. When he came to rest, he saw one of the figures staggering about, hunched up slightly and apparently clutching an injured shoulder. His horse was hazing away up the trail. The second figure was still clutching the bridle of his mount, but Conant saw the outline of his rifle in his hand, being raised to his shoulder, levelled in the direction of the position from which the man on the ground first fired. Conant fired first. The man with the rifle shrieked and pitched forward on his face, dropping the weapon.

The second and horseless man went running for the other's animal as Mead Conant raised himself to his knees.

The wounded man grabbed the horse and mounted. The animal was between him and Conant and when the wounded man was in the saddle, he wheeled the horse at once, presenting his back to the big man kneeling in the gritty shale.

Conant held his fire. He had never yet shot a man in the back and had no intention of turning back-shooter now, even in the case of this unknown dry-gulch rifleman.

He pegged a parting shot after the fleeing rider as he rose to his full length, firing high to throw a scare into the mounted man. The dwindling rider swivelled in the saddle and a six-gun cracked from his hand. Considering that it was fired from a running horse and in darkness, the shot was a lucky one. Mead Conant felt a burning bite gnaw into the flesh of his upper left arm. He raised his uninjured arm to fire at the mounted man, but he had already been swallowed by the night.

'All right, *hombre*,' he grunted in the direction of the diminishing hoofbeats, 'I hit you in the shoulder. I'll know you again!'

The wound in his arm started to throb dully, but the bone seemed to be intact. Conant holstered his Colts and walked up the trail to where the crumpled form of the second man lay. As he stooped over the corpse, the high-riding moon sailed out from behind a cloudbank to illuminate the form of a small, stocky man in worn range-garb, lying on his face. Conant turned the body over. His shot had taken the bushwhacker clean through the forehead.

The dead man was round-faced and had a thick stubble of beard on his chin. There was nothing about the moon-illumed features that reminded Conant of anyone he had known in these parts in his younger days.

A footfall sounded behind the crouching man. He shot upwards like an uncoiling spring, whirling about and drawing his right-hand Colt at the same time.

'Don't shoot, mister,' said a voice.

Conant saw a slim figure coming up the darkened trail, with his hands held high to show he had no weapon. Conant held his pose, with the six-gun still levelled at the newcomer, who continued walking slowly up-trail until Conant was able to discern him as a lean, gangling man in his early twenties. He wore a woollen shirt, an old leather vest and scuffed jeans. There was an ancient Smith & Wesson five-shooter holstered at his belt. The very way he wore it denoted the fact that he was no gun-hand. He didn't look a cowman, either.

'I was comin' up the trail when I heard shots. I would have given you some help after I heard who was shootin' at you, but you seemed to be doin' all right by yourself – I ain't much of a shot, anyway,' said the youngster.

Conant shoved his gun into leather in the face of the young man's frank approach.

'What do you mean, you heard who was shootin' at me?' he asked.

'I heard the voice say you'd been hit. That was Cliff Dignan's voice, he's foreman of the Flying Spur.'

The name stirred a half-forgotten chord in Conant. He remembered Dignan from when he had been a kid. Dignan had been with the Flying Spur riders the night they swooped on the Conant homestead.

The young man jerked his head towards the dead man on the trail.

'That's Spade Lacy,' he said. 'He's another of Arch Tamblyn's gunnies.'

Conant eyed the shadowed face of the younger man.

'If you intended comin' in against Tamblyn's men, you must have a grudge against the Flying Spur,' he observed. 'I thought Tamblyn had about cleaned up all opposition by now.'

'Not all. There's some of us nesters up at North Ridge that he's been crowdin' for some time. Things ain't got real bad yet, but I figure they will sooner or later. My name's Dave Apsley, by the way.'

'Mine's Mead Conant,' said the other.

He saw Apsley's eyes widen.

'Conant!' he repeated. 'You're Conant the—' He paused uncertainly.

'Yeah – the gunslinger,' finished Conant, stretching out his right hand.

Dave Apsley took it with a noticeable eagerness.

'You're hit,' he observed. 'Maybe you'll come up to my cabin an' we'll get that slug out of you an' you can have a bite of supper.'

'Glad to,' agreed Conant. 'Homesteader folks is my kind of folks. I didn't think there would be any left around here.'

'Just four families of us up in the North Ridge region. We've only been there since the spring. Homestead Act says we can settle there.'

'But Arch Tamblyn says different, eh?'

'Yeah. He sent Cliff Dignan out soon after we settled in to tell us we had until the Fall to pull out. He said nobody would be hurt until September the first and we could stay on what he claimed was his land until that date, but if we are still there on September first, Flying Spur will blast us off.'

'Sounds like Arch Tamblyn is gettin' considerate in his old age,' mused Conant as they mounted their horses. 'He never gave my old man and my brothers a time-limit to get off Moroni Creek where he claimed he had water-rights.'

'Yeah, we heard about that,' Apsley said. 'Flying Spur riders kind of throw that in our faces when we meet up with them. "You better think about pullin' up yore stakes off Flying Spur land, or you'll likely wind up like the Conant boys", they say.'

Mead Conant inched his mouth into a hard smile.

'Could be that a lot of folks will wind up like the Conant boys before long,' he said half to himself.

They headed their horses' noses northward and rode in silence for several minutes.

'September the first, you said,' mused Conant, still

half to himself, 'and today is August fifth. Is anyone up in your direction showin' any sign of weakening?'

'We're all kinda jittery, but holdin' on with a weak bravado,' Dave Apsley admitted. 'We know we don't stand a chance against the Flying Spur outfit. I guess someone'll sneak off before Tamblyn's time limit is up an' the rest'll just naturally follow.'

'But the Homestead Act says you have a right to settle on free land,' Conant said. 'Seems to me I'll spend some time loafin' around North Ridge, since I came back to these parts to make trouble for the Flying Spur, anyway.'

'You mean you came alone for that purpose?' asked the youngster riding beside him.

'Yeah, but Tamblyn seems to have gotten word I was around, even though I circled Huajillo so I wouldn't be seen. Don't make a powerful lot of difference, anyway; he'll get to know I'm really an' truly around right soon.'

TWO

Dave Apsley's homestead up at North Ridge was about the same as every homestead Mead Conant ever knew. There was the usual air of general untidiness – a mark of the man who was trying to make a farm out of wild land – about the place. A little crop-garden stood off to one side of the new-looking wooden shack and a small barn stood at its back.

In a lot of ways it reminded Conant of the place his father and brothers built down beside Moroni Creek.

Yellow lamp-light bloomed from a chintz-curtained window of the cabin.

Apsley and Conant swung down from their saddles, the young nester taking a gunny-sack from the rear of his cantle as he did so.

'Supplies,' he explained. 'I went into Huajillo to get them. I was comin' back when I heard them *hombres* shootin' at you.'

They tethered their horses in the tiny barn and walked around to the cabin door. Apsley knocked lightly.

'It's Dave, Mildred,' he called.

The sound of a bolt being drawn back came from the other side of the door which swung back to reveal the trim figure of a girl, in plain homestead woman's dress, framed in the lamp-light backed portal. Because the light was behind her, Conant could not see the girl's face, but her hair, clouding about her head, looked like spun gold.

'I brought a friend back, Mildred. He's had a little accident. Meet Mead Conant. Mead, this is my sister, Mildred.'

Conant swept his sombrero from his head and heard the girl gasp at the mention of his name. He wondered how bad his reputation was. He was not a wanton gunslinger; most of his reputation had been earned as an officer of the law, but, with his kind, people added to what they knew about him so that he might well appear to be more bad man than good. At the same time he felt mildly surprised that the blonde girl was Apsley's sister. He had imagined her to be his wife.

He waited to see if the girl proffered her hand. She did and he shook it. A work-hardened hand, but still gentle.

Dave Apsley ushered him into the cabin. It was simply, but comfortably, furnished. In the lamplight he saw that Apsley's sister was astonishingly lovely in a simple and unadorned way.

Apsley settled the guest into a chair while the girl hastened to the tiny kitchen built off the main room of the homestead.

'I'll get hot water,' she announced.

Conant rolled up the bullet-slashed sleeve of his

shirt and examined the wound. The slug had passed clear through the flesh and, while the wound was painful, it was not serious.

Mildred Apsley appeared with hot water and some strips of cloth. She and her brother cleaned and bandaged the wound. When it was done, Conant stood up and flexed his arm, then moved it up and down a number of times. The injury would not impair his gunspeed with his left hand and he counted his ability to draw both guns quickly as a most important factor now he was back in the Flying Spur territory.

Mildred busied herself in the kitchen again and soon spread the table with meat, potatoes, biscuits and coffee. Conant sat down and ate heartily, finding the food a great deal more palatable than that he had bought in the Tombstone eating-house.

When Conant finished eating, he realized self-consciously that he was still wearing his guns. Eating with a gun-heavy belt buckled about him was a habit formed in his days as a town marshal. It had stuck with the growth of his gun-fighting reputation – an increasing reputation brought the danger of 'rep-seekers' trying to gun him in the back.

Once or twice he caught the girl casting glances towards him, half fearful glances; peaceable people often looked at him that way when the mark of the gunslinger was showing particularly bold upon him.

After the meal, Apsley stuffed tobacco into a corncob pipe while Conant rolled a ricepaper smoke. They smoked in silence for a while. It was a silence that accrued weight as it lengthened; each had something to say but they would not speak while the girl was in the background clearing away the dishes. Eventually she went into the small kitchen.

Conant faced the homesteader over the empty table, taking the measure of his youthful but resolute features through the haze of smoke. He looked as if he might turn into a fighting man if he had to.

The gunslinger jerked his head towards the door, indicating the outside world in general.

'These homesteader neighbours of yours, will they make a stand against the Flyin' Spur if someone leads 'em? Would they back up a man who set himself square against Tamblyn's slug-slingers, or would they run when the shootin' started?'

Apsley eyed the lean gunfighter with a certain determination mirrored on his face.

'Funny you should ask that, Mead. I was just thinkin' along those lines myself. I was wonderin', you comin' back here to make trouble for Tamblyn, the way you have, maybe you can put some fightin' spirit into the homesteaders. Right now, they're hangin' on to their land, but Arch Tamblyn's time-limit is drawin' near – someone's bound to sneak off sooner or later an' that'll stampede all the rest.'

'Yeah,' drawled Conant thoughtfully. 'I wouldn't like to see you folks get the kind of deal my old man and brothers were handed by Tamblyn, but the Homestead Act says you can settle on this land an' Tamblyn has no right to haze you off it. You say there are four families up here on North Ridge?'

'Yeah. Three more besides Mildred an' me.'

'Fellers with wives an' kids?'

'Two of 'em have. The third homestead is owned by

two bachelor brothers, Seth an' Bill Diffin. I guess Seth an' Bill will make a stand against the Flyin' Spur, if they have someone to give 'em confidence. I can't speak for the others, you know how it is when a man has a wife an' family.'

'Yeah,' nodded Conant. 'How about you an' your sister? Would you back a man who shoved his gunfightin' reputation down Arch Tamblyn's throat?'

Dave Apsley's face set into hard lines.

'We would for sure, Mead, both of us. We worked hard to come out here from the East. We wanted to build something worthwhile for ourselves an' live where the air is fit to breathe. We'll back you, Mead.'

'Good,' praised the gunfighter. 'I'm not settin' myself up as a hired gunhand, Dave. I had no notion you nesters were out here when I came back to this country, but if I can stop Tamblyn from runnin' you off your land while I'm in the process of squarin' with this outfit for the killin' of my father an' brothers, I will. I'll see his gunhands don't treat you the way they treated my folks, but there's one thing that's plumb essential in a fight like this an' that's unity. You homestead folk will have to stick together in the face of Tamblyn's threats. If one family runs for the tall timber when the goin' looks tough, the rest will be demoralized an' they'll probably follow. Think we can talk 'em into stickin' together?'

'We can try,' declared the nester with enthusiasm.

There was the rawness of autumn in the dawn of the following day when Mead Conant and Dave ApsIcy rode the saddleback of North Ridge. The red flushes of the new day washed up against a cold sky. The distant desert mesas, away to the south, were rugged studs standing against the chill sweeps of the wide sky.

The riders angled down a narrow trail which ribboned down the ridge side and reached the Diffin place first.

There was nothing special about it. It was a cramped homestead and the stark light of dawn slanted across its yard to pick out an untidiness that pointed to the fact that a woman's influence was missing. The homestead had the usual crop patch and a small, lean-to barn as well as a wooden, half-faced structure which sheltered a couple of scrubby horses. The pole and lath outbuildings huddled around the homestead cabin in its trash and tin-can littered yard and the whole place had a general air of clinging to the ridge side in hopeless desperation.

Conant and Apsley rode into the yard, pulled rein at the door of the cabin, and Apsley knocked without dismounting. The door creaked open and framed a small man, bald-headed, unshaven and with sleep in his eyes. He wore a grubby red undershirt and a pair of scuffed jeans. He looked at the two horsemen with wrinkle-fringed eyes.

'Why, Dave! What're you doin' here this early?' he queried when he recognized Apsley.

'Bill, this is Mead Conant,' introduced Apsley, jerking his head towards the tall rider at his side. 'You've heard of him, I guess.'

Bill Diffin's stubbled jaw slackened open when he heard the name. His eyes widened on the tall, wide-hatted horseman on whose rugged features the spreading dawn painted rosy hues.

'Sure, I heard of him,' breathed the little home-steader.

'He came back here to square up with Tamblyn's outfit for the way his kin was killed back on Moroni Creek twelve years ago. He'll put some shots in on our account, if we back him up.'

Bill Diffin's eyebrows slid up towards his bald dome. He compressed his lips and looked at Mead Conant steadily. He took in the big Colts, the cartridge-garnished gunbelts, the thongs that tied the holsters down to the lean, jean-clad legs of the gunfighter. His gaze rested for a while on the hard features under the sweep of the sombrero brim, noting the premature wrinkles of bitter experience around Conant's mouth. Finally he said: 'Is he lookin' for money for it?' It was a question asked of Dave Apsley, but Diffin was staring directly into Conan's face as he asked it.

Conant slewed himself around in the saddle slightly to face Bill Diffin. It was he who answered the question.

'I ain't lookin' for money. I have a personal fight against Arch Tamblyn an' I'll act for you folks because you're my kind of people. All I want is to be sure that you'll stick together when Tamblyn's crew start throwin' lead – because that's what they'll do. Homesteaders can't fight cattlemen alone, they have to fight together. My old man an' my brothers tried to stand alone twelve years ago an' they were butchered.'

That seemed to satisfy Bill Diffin. He turned his head and called: 'Seth,' into the dark portal of the shack. A sleepy grunt answered and, after a second or two, a lean figure in a nightshirt presented itself at his back. Seth Diffin was the opposite of his brother. He was tall with a shock of tangled black hair. Even at this early hour, when he had been dragged from his bed, he had a certain cheerfulness about his thin features.

'This is Mead Conant, the gunfighter,' introduced his brother flatly. 'He's come to make fight with Arch Tamblyn for what the Flying Spur gunnies did to his old man an' brothers years ago. Wants to put in a few slugs for us homesteaders. Do we join him?'

Seth's features were split by a wide grin.

'Do we?' he repeated. 'I'll say we do, Bill. We'll fight with you, Conant. Me an' Bill ain't anythin' special as gunmen, but we can handle our weapons tolerable well. Right glad you stopped by, somethin' like you is what we need around here.'

And that seemed to be that. Conant thought he had the Diffin brothers well figured. Bill was the shrewd one, the one who wanted to know if the gunfighter was selling his trigger-skill into the homesteader trouble on the Spanish Saddle range. Seth was less calculating, a man with more gusto, probably far more happy-go-lucky. He figured both brothers were reliable.

'We can depend on 'em,' Dave Apsley told Conant as they rode out of the Diffins' yard. 'Next place up the ridge is Carl Quillan's. He has a wife an' a slew of youngsters. Can't say how he'll feel about a stand-up fight with Tamblyn.'

They rode into the blossoming day and came to Quillan's place in a little less than an hour of riding.

The yard was much neater than that of the last outfit they had visited. In the brassy morning sunlight, Carl Quillan was repairing the tail-board of a small buggy off to one side of the house. A woman of perhaps twenty-five, with a small baby in her arms and two older children clinging to her skirts appeared in the doorway of the shack. She was girlish and pretty although a little peaked.

Apsley said, 'Morning, Becky,' as both men rode past the shack, touching their hats. Conant did not fail to see Quillan's wife bite her lip suddenly as she looked at him. It reminded him of the glances Mildred Apsley bestowed on him the previous evening. Bitterly, he reflected that he must have 'gunfighter' written all over him without realising it.

Carl Quillan had straightened up from his hammering at the new tail-board on the buggy at the approach of the two riders. He stood now watching them inquisitively as they drew upon him and pulled rein. He was about the same age as his wife and still much of a gangling boy. His eyes were blue and frank in a face reddened by harsh Arizona days. He had sandy hair, cultivated down the sides of his cheeks in the fashion of the dandies of the period.

Without dismounting, Apsley introduced Conant and put the question of Quillan's loyalty in the event of a stand-up fight with the Flying Spur to him as flatly as he had to Bill Diffin.

Quillan studied the ground and scraped a toe in the dust awkwardly.

'It's difficult to say, Dave,' he stated in a husky drawl. 'I got Becky an' the kids to consider. Can't say I want to run them into any gun-trouble. If it was just myself, I'd be with you, but it's Becky an' the kids.' He straightened his narrow shoulders and faced Conant squarely. 'I don't want the thing that happened to your folk on Moroni Creek to happen to my kin,' he declared. 'Fact is, me an' Becky more or less decided to pull out soon. The only reason we waited this long is because we thought Arch Tamblyn might be bluffin' about that time limit.'

Mead Conant canted his long body forward in his saddle, rested his hands on the horn and said flatly:

'One thing you can be sure of, Quillan: Arch Tamblyn wasn't bluffin' when he said he'd run you off North Ridge if you didn't pull up stakes an' travel by September first. I'll tell you somethin' else that's plumb certain sure, though: the Flyin' Spur gunnies won't do to your folks what they did to mine – I promise that!'

The gunfighter and the nester faced each other in silence for a long instant, then, in more friendly tones, Conant said: 'You've got a good wife an' cute kids, Carl, an' you've made a decent place for them here by damned hard work. It's all too good to be trampled under the feet of the Flyin' Spur cow-critters. Stand by your neighbours an' Tamblyn's cattle will never run on land the government says is yours. Think about it, Carl.'

They rode out of the homestead leaving Quillan standing in the sunlight, watching their retreating backs. The homesteader's wife was still in the doorway of the shack with the baby and the other children.

Conant was disturbed. He didn't blame a man for

thinking of his family first, but he didn't want to see any of these North Ridge nesters weakening and running for the tall timber, giving Tamblyn the chance of running his stock over the land they had struggled to cultivate. There was no telling with a fellow like Quillan. He had confessed that he was almost ready to run from the ridge. If he did his action could only demoralize the remaining nesters and weaken their chances against the Flying Spur.

When the sun was high, slamming its power out of the wide, azure sky, Conant and Apsley reached the third homestead, Gerry Hannaway's, at the northern end of the ridge.

Hannaway's place was less neat than Quillan's, yet a considerable cut above the bedraggled bachelor holding of the Diffin brothers. Gerry Hannaway was the oldest of the North Ridge homesteaders, turned fifty, but his wife was younger and his family, two boys and a girl, were approaching maturity. Hannaway asked the visitors into his shack and his wife prepared coffee for them. She discreetly left the men alone in the main room of the dwelling and busied herself in the yard where the two youths were repairing some harness and the girl was milking the family cow.

Hannaway listened to Apsley and Conant in grim silence. He had lined features of a peculiarly Lincolnesque cast and his mouth was set in a tight line. He listened to his visitors' talk of war against Arch Tamblyn in silence until they had finished.

'I'll back you,' he promised promptly. 'I don't have to consider it or think about it, I'll back you! I'm older than you men an' I claim I have a right to government land. I fought in the war an' I got shot up at First Bull Run an' got shot up again at Chancellorsville. I had damned little before the war an' not much more after it, for all I was on the winnin' side. Now, I've got this little place, an' I aim to keep it. Besides, Tamblyn's made it clear in the past that he hates me 'cause I served in the Yankee army. I figure I'll relish standin' against him!'

Mead Conant quirked his lips into a hard smile.

'Good to hear you talk like that, Gerry,' he said. 'That's the way my old man used to talk, full of old soldier fire an' brimstone. He was an old Confederate, same as Tamblyn, but Tamblyn had no sentiment about his old comrades-in-arms when he loosed his killers on Moroni Creek. That won't happen on North Ridge. Stand your ground an' you'll see Arch Tamblyn climb down some in the near future.'

Apsley and Conant rode off the Hannaway holding considerably heartened by the determined attitude of Gerry Hannaway. Conant rode in silence, thinking that Quillan was the only apparent weakness in the North Ridge homesteaders' opposition to the Flying Spur. His thoughts took another trend and, as they approached the Apsley homestead when the sun was reaching its mid-day zenith, a course of action that had been suggesting itself to him since early that morning solidified into determination.

As the pair came angling down the dusty ridge on sidestepping mounts, a pencil of grey smoke rose plumb against the sun-whitened blue of the sky from the stovepipe of the Apsley place.

'Mildred will have a meal ready for us,' Apsley said.

'I didn't ask you before, Mead, but you'll stay with us for a while, won't you? We have room enough for you an' we're right glad to have you.'

'Thanks,' said Conant. 'I'll stay, sure, an' I appreciate yore kindness. Would you make an excuse to Mildred for me an' ask her to hold the meal over for me a little while? I want to go down to Moroni Creek an' then over to the Flyin' Spur. I guess I'll be back around mid-afternoon.'

'To the Flyin' Spur?' echoed Apsley. 'You goin' there alone? What for?'

'I want to see Arch Tamblyn's noble features — under certain circumstances,' replied the gunfighter with a tight little smile.

'Is it safe to go alone — should I come with you?' asked Apsley. Half-way through the question he realized that the man riding beside him had a big reputation as a gun-hand, while he was no kind of gun-hand at all. There was nothing patronizing in Mead Conant's answer.

'No. Stay around home with Mildred,' he said. 'I'll be back before long.'

He thumped his knees into his horse's ribs and moved off down the ridge, riding at a steady jog. Dave Apsley watched him go, the dry, red dust pluming lazily in his back-trail. He rode with an erect and alert bearing, the tatters of the sleeve that was ripped by the bullet of the would-be assassin of the previous night fluttering in the slight breeze. The sun touched bright points to his gun-gear as he rode down the ridge and made the bone handles of his twin Colts the most conspicuous feature of the lean rider.

Apsley remembered how he'd been in Tombstone once when Wyatt Earp, erstwhile marshal of that town, came riding down the street with a face of thunder to face a bunch of malcontents at the far end of the town. The law-man had moved his horse along at the same steady gait. There was the same alertness to the man in the saddle and the same prominence of twin guns as he now saw in Mead Conant's dwindling form.

There was a distinct hallmark on the sight: a gunfighter riding!

Three

As he expected, Mead Conant found the body of Spade Lacy stiffened on the trail where the Flying Spur bushwhacker met his end the previous night. The vultures had been busy on it and two of the ugly birds flapped away with ominously rustling wings as Conant's horse approached.

The gunfighter pulled his steed to a halt, swung down from the saddle and hoisted the stiff, vulture-ravaged corpse over the neck of the horse. He climbed into his saddle, spurred up the bronc into a smart clip and headed for the Flying Spur headquarters with his grisly burden.

Rather more than an hour of steady riding brought him to the arched gate of the ranch. He went through it at a walk, the stiff corpse of Lacy draped over the forepart of the saddle.

Arch Tamblyn's ranch was typical of the desert-edge outfits of the South-west. The house was made of adobe with an overtone of Spanish influence in its architecture. Around it, in an untidy clutter, were ranged the bunkhouse, a couple of barns, a thatched cookshack and a number of pole-fenced corrals. The wide yard of the Flying Spur headquarters was wheel-scored and pocked by hooves and bootheels.

A drift of smoke from the canted and rusted stovepipe of the cook-shack hazed lazily across the sun-splashed yard. The half-dozen punchers who had been engaged on various chores around the yard paused in their work and stood like so many big-hatted statues, watching Conant enter the yard with the corpse slung across his mount.

The gunfighter rode, straight-backed, past them, ignoring them as if they did not exist and heading for the ranchhouse. A Mexican in a sugar-loaf hat and serape was standing close to the steps of the gallery which ran the length of the front of the house. He watched Conant ride towards the building with wide, jet eyes.

Conant danced his horse nearer to the steps of the gallery. From under its hooves, dry flurries of dust spurted up and lingered for a long time on the hot air.

The gunfighter pulled rein facing the front of the gallery and the arched doorway of the house.

'Tell Tamblyn I want to see him,' he ordered the Mexican curtly.

The Mexican jumped out of his frozen attitude.

'Don't bother,' grated a voice with a noticeable Texas drawl. 'I'm here!'

Arch Tamblyn came out of the gloomy interior of the house, strutting like a fighting-cock, paunchy, old, but supple, alert and dangerous. He wore bullet stud-ded gun gear around his middle and a Colt .45 rode low against his right hip. The rancher halted on the gallery, facing the mounted man in the yard. At Conant's back, the Flying Spur riders held their frozen positions.

There was an oddly silent moment during which Cliff Dignan, with his left arm in a sling, came around one corner of the house. Mead Conant saw him appear and halt in his tracks with a corner of his eye.

On the gallery of the ranch-house, Arch Tamblyn held a stiff pose with his legs wide apart.

'What're you doing here, Conant. . . ?' he began.

'I'll do the talkin',' cut in Conant. He yanked the body of Spade Lacy up from its position across the fore of his saddle and allowed it to slither stiffly down to the ground. It flopped heavily to the dust and lay before the steps of the gallery with the vulture-ravaged face staring up at the tyrant sun.

'You sent this man to kill me last night, Tamblyn, an' I'm bringing him back,' Conant said in flat tones. 'Next time you try to bushwhack me, send someone who can perform the chore. I also came to tell you that I aim to finish your land-grab notions about the homesteads on North Ridge. You won't be drivin' anybody off North Ridge after September first or at any other time. In addition, I intend to square with you an' the *hombres* who killed my father an' brothers twelve years ago. Some of them are in this yard now an' I remember the faces of the others. If you want trouble now, Tamblyn, you can grab for yore gun. You an' yore murderers can either take my bullets in yore yellow guts now, or wait for 'em — it don't make much difference to me, 'cause you'll get 'em eventually!'

Tamblyn had been staring at the sprawled corpse of Spade Lacy. He raised his eyes now and glowered at Mead Conant scornfully.

'You talk powerful big, Conant,' he grated. 'Powerful big for a man that's alone.'

Conant's eyes became screwed-up slits as he answered flatly and with a calculated deliberation:

'I can back my talk, Tamblyn. Don't make the mistake of thinkin' I can't.'

Arch Tamblyn watched the lean, bleak-eyed face of Mead Conant and something stirred deep in his innards. It was something he had never known before, but he recognised it for what it was – fear. The scornful expression died on the rancher's face as he stood staring at the mounted man who faced him. Conant was sitting his saddle easily, lean brown hands crossed on the pommel.

The Flying Spur hands stood around in their frozen positions. A hot, spiralling wind whisked in off the desert-range and sent flurries of dust eddying across the ranch-yard. From where Cliff Dignan stood, there came a swift action. Swift in the eyes of the other watchers, but Mead Conant saw it with the tail of his gunfighter's eye; it was slow, clumsy and utterly stupid. The action was telegraphed to Conant's brain in an immeasurably small amount of time.

Cliff Dignan, going for his gun with his good hand.

The watchers scarcely saw Conant's hands move from the saddle pommel, but they were suddenly gripping his twin Colts, Colts that were blazing spurts of flame and slamming out a deafening roar that clattered over the sun-pounded ranch-yard and off across

the desert range. Cliff Dignan reeled back against the
adobe wall of the house. His gun was clear of leather
and a reflex action of his finger triggered a slug into
the dust as he went spinning off-balance.

Through the swirl of cordite smoke, the Flying
Spur's foreman was visible as a twitching dummy, an
expression of stark horror fixed on his face.

Conant's horse reared when the shooting started.

The gunfighter sensed hostility at his back, twisted
himself around in the bucking saddle, and had a
whirling glimpse of one of the cowhands across the
yard with a naked gun in his hand. Conant blazed a
shot and the man with the gun teetered forward,
crumpled at the knees and slumped into the dust. The
remaining Flying Spur riders froze into stiff positions
once more.

Conant used his knees to bring the fractious horse
under control and faced Arch Tamblyn again. The
rancher was standing in a strangely twisted attitude,
on the gallery, his right hand held out in an arrested
clawing motion over the butt of his Colt.

Off by the corner of the ranch-house, Cliff
Dignan's body, which had been slumped against the
building, slithered down into the powdery dust, leaving a red smear on the dingy white of the adobe wall.
In the sunlight, gunsmoke hazed over the yard in flat
drifts.

Conant knew the men at his back would not
attempt to draw on him; they stood awed by his swift
gunplay. He knew, too, that Arch Tamblyn would make
no effort to go through with his draw. Standing on the
gallery, the owner of the Flying Spur spread contem-

plated the whipcord-lean rider with eyes that were wide with amazement, eyes that mirrored not a little fear.

With a measure of contempt in the action, Mead Conant sheathed his left-hand gun in its holster and grabbed his rein with the free hand.

'Don't forget what I said about the homesteaders, Tamblyn,' he reminded the rancher. 'You won't be runnin' anybody off any land.'

Tamblyn's brown, proud-veined hand flopped to his side limply. The gunfighter kept his ice-bleak eyes on the big-moustached cattleman for an instant of silence, then he yanked his bronc around and steered it at a walk for the arched gateway, still with a naked gun in his right hand. Without turning his head, he called back to Tamblyn:

'If you've got a man in this outfit who thinks he can plug me in the back as I ride out, he's welcome to try!'

No one tried. The Flying Spur hands watched him ride out of the gateway in awed silence. They remembered the stories that travelled along the frontier, stories telling of Mead Conant's trigger-skill. He was hell on wheels with a gun, they said. There was no denying it, he was everything the stories claimed. He must have eyes in the back of his head, the way he whirled around in the saddle when there was danger at his back.

He was hell on wheels all right. He rode into the Flying Spur yard with a corpse over his bronc and rode out again leaving two more stiffening in the blood-pooled dust.

There was contempt for the owner of the ranch and

his riders contained in Conant's attitude as he rode off the Flying Spur.

He did not look back once.

Four

Evening was sifting down over the spiny land when the clatter of boots and the ring of spurs sounded from the gallery of the Flying Spur ranch-house. Arch Tamblyn, sitting close to the empty field-stone fire-place of the main room of the building, looked up to see four of his hands trooping in, dragging their feet as if reluctant to enter. They were all old Flying Spur hands: Jeff Kersands, Shorty Wilkes, Whitey Heldkopf and Cal Millick. Kersands, as the oldest of the bunch, moved a little shamefacedly to the fore.

There was much about the manner of these hard-faced cowhands that reminded Tamblyn of so many scared children. He sensed trouble and his longhorn moustache positively bristled.

'Well?' he demanded. 'What do you want?'

Jeff Kensands studied the boards of the floor uncertainly. He did not look at the rancher as he started to speak.

'Arch, we – er – these boys an' me, we—' he faltered. Then he braced his body and blurted the words out. 'We want our time, Arch, we're quittin'!'

The owner of the Flying Spur leapt to his feet, his wrinkled, mahogany coloured face twisted in unbelieving rage.

'Quittin'!' he exploded. 'Why, you boys have been here for years!' The rancher stood rooted to the spot, opening and closing his big fists in rage. The four cowboys stood before him, heads drooping.

'It's Conant, ain't it?' bellowed Tamblyn. 'He rode into my yard, dumped what was left of Spade Lacy on my doorstep, and shot Dignan an' Schneeman. It's that damned, gun-hung Conant that's put quittin' into yore heads, ain't it?'

'We don't want to quit, Arch,' began Kersands lamely.

'But you're askin' for yore time, just the same,' thundered the old Texan. 'You saw that Conant hellion in action an' you're scared!'

'It's not that we want to run out, Arch,' Whitey Heldkopf put in, his voice quavering slightly. 'But Conant's got a big reputation, an' now we've seen what he can do with his guns. You heard what he said about squarin' up with those who were on Moroni Creek the nights his brothers an' old man were killed. We were there, Arch, an' that was twelve years back – we ain't so slick with our triggers these days, we're all older men . . .'

'You're a pack of yeller, Gentle Annies,' bawled Tamblyn. 'I'll lick Conant an' his big trigger-rep yet! One man rides into my yard an' my crew starts hazin' – all on account of one man!'

Shorty Wilkes shoved his black-stubbled jaw forward truculently.

'I didn't notice you goin' through with yore draw on

the gallery, Arch,' he stated calmly.

The rancher glowered at Wilkes, showing his yellowed teeth like an angered dog.

'Get out, the whole damned bunch of you!' he growled. 'Come back in an hour an' I'll give you yore blamed time. I got no use for yeller bellies!'

The punchers marched out, trailing their spurs. Tamblyn stood for a moment, opening and closing his fists in that gesture of desperate agitation, then he crossed to a small cabinet and produced a whiskey bottle and a glass. He poured himself a stiff three fingers, downed it and spilled more whiskey into the glass. From here, he could see the ranch-yard through the window and the figures of the four men who had just faced him trudging across it towards he dusk-gloomed bunkhouse.

'Quitters!' he grunted into his glass.

It made a man want to heave up his guts. Four men running from one!

In spite of the warmth of the liquor, Arch Tamblyn felt that chill stirring deep in his innards again, that same unnerving qualm he had known when Mead Conant faced him earlier that day. The truth was that four of the gunhands Tamblyn gathered about him in the days when he was building the Flying Spread empire with blood and bullets were running from the nester kid who came back pushing a big reputation before him. After that display of slug-slamming in the yard of the Flying Spur, the whole crew would probably want to run for the tall timber before long and the fact that Kersands, Millick, Wilkes and Heldkopf were quitting would hasten the process.

Tamblyn slammed his glass down on the cabinet top decisively.

He would have to do something damned quick, or the might of Flying Spur would collapse around his ears.

He didn't want to be left without gunhands around him. He was getting to be an old man.

Also, he was getting to be scared.

It was late and the white moon was riding high when Seth Diffin pulled his horse to a halt outside Dave Apsley's homestead. The lanky nester swung down from his saddle with a certain joyous air and made his long-legged way to the cabin from the windows of which lamplight splashed in yellow rays.

Diffin hit the latch and shoved the door open without concerning himself with the formality of knocking. He found Apsley, his sister and Mead Conant over supper. A wide grin split the homely features of the gangling homesteader as he marched into the cabin.

'Nice shootin,' Mead,' he greeted. 'I'm just on my way back from Huajillo. While I was in Heenan's store, four of Tamblyn's gunnies came in. They told Heenan they were pulling out of the Spanish Saddle country – quittin' Tamblyn's outfit. I heard 'em talkin' about you ridin' into the Flyin' Spur yard, throwin' what was left of Spade Lacy on the gallery step an' shooting Dignan when he clawed for his iron. Them fellers were plumb scared, Mead. They're pullin' out before you cross their trail again.'

An uneasy silence settled on the small homestead as Diffin finished his enthusiastic account. Conant saw Apsley watching him with his jaw sagging open. On the far side of the table, Mildred's face was shocked and horror was mirrored in her eyes.

'So that's what you went off on your lonesome to do?' murmured Dave Apsley.

Mildred stood up suddenly. Conant saw the lamp-light put a glitter on a tear in her eye as she rushed for the door in a rustle of skirts, running into the open air and slamming the door behind her.

Seth Diffin regarded the door in puzzlement.

'What's the matter with her?' he husked. 'Somethin' I said upset her?'

'I don't know,' confessed Apsley awkwardly as he rose to his feet and made a move for the door. 'I never saw her act that way before.'

Conant stood up quickly and reached the door before Apsley.

'It ain't so much what you said, Seth as what I did,' he told the visiting homesteader. He yanked the door open and strode into the night.

He found Mildred standing close to the small barn with her back to him. The moon touched white points to her golden. hair; her shoulders were heaving slightly. Conant stood a little distance from her.

'I'm sorry,' he said softly. 'You have to do that kind of thing when you're dealin' with Arch Tamblyn's kind.'

The girl whirled around to face him, her cheeks wet with tears.

'Sorry!' she mocked. 'It's too awful to think about – what you did at the Flying Spur! I should have known what you were. I had enough warning the night Dave brought you home – you didn't even take off your guns when you sat down to supper! You're a killer – as much a killer as any of those gun-carrying hands on Tamblyn's ranch!'

Mead Conant felt something like an icy knife drive through his whole being as he looked into the angry tearstained face of the girl. He clenched his hands into tight fists. It was hell trying to understand the workings of a woman's mind; he was a long way off his range, in a situation like this. He was conscious of a vague hurt inside him.

'Listen,' he said hoarsely. 'This is tough territory and you have to be tough to survive in it. You have to show men like Tamblyn that you can be tough, or his kind'll shoot you down an' trample their horses over what's left of you – I know, I've seen it! I know what Tamblyn can do; I saw it when I was a kid. My father and brothers weren't the first nesters the Flying Spur gunned off Moroni Creek, either. There were a couple of Mormon families there, before we came, it was they who named the creek after the angel in the Book of Mormon. The name stuck, but the Mormons didn't – Tamblyn ran 'em off like jackrabbits. He'd do it here at North Ridge, too, but I aim to show him bullets before he gets to startin'.'

Mildred Apsley was still regarding him with scorn in her tear-dimmed eyes.

'You're no better than any other gunfighter,' she husked. 'Your grudge against Tamblyn has made you into a killer. I sensed that you were bringing trouble when you walked into the cabin for the first time – you and your big gunfighting reputation – you're just a killer!'

Conant was conscious of the dim hurt inside him throbbing with intensified pain.

'I never killed a man who didn't need killin', he stated flatly.

'But they were men, weren't they – what right have you to transform human beings into notches on your guns?'

'No!' rasped Conant harshly. 'They were not men – they might have been once, but they weren't men when I gunned them down! They were dangerous animals! I don't keep notches on my guns, but I'll name the animals you called men: there was Charlie Van Donck, who shot at least five men, mostly in the back; Harvey Clyde, a trigger-happy lunatic who'd shoot a woman or a child if the mood was on him; Ace Banselling—'

'Stop!' Mildred's voice had a shrill edge to it; she clenched her slender hands tight and pressed them to her mouth. 'Stop! I don't want to hear about them!'

Conant said, in a softer tone:

'There were plenty others, all of the same breed. I was wearing a lawman's badge every time I pulled a trigger; I was elected by decent people to deal with lawbreakers. Those men had to be killed or they'd go on to commit murder after murder. I had to kill them the same way your brother would have to kill a lobo wolf if one got into your crops.'

Without another word, the slender girl turned about and made for the cabin. Her brother and Seth Diffin, standing in the light-backed open door, moved silently and awkwardly aside to let her pass, then they walked slowly over to the tall figure of the gunfighter.

Seth Diffin studied the dark ground.

'I figure I should have kept my mouth shut about what you did at the Flyin' Spur, Mead,' he rumbled. 'I didn't think it would upset her that way.'

'She'll get over it,' Apsley said. 'She finds it hard to get used to this territory sometimes – so do I for that matter. It's so big an' beautiful, but so violent it makes you scared. It's tougher on Mildred. She spent a long time at school back in the east an' it made her kind of genteel; she kind of forgets life ain't so ladylike out here.'

'You don't have to make excuses for her,' Conant said sharply. 'She's right. Killin' a man is a dirty business, an' what I did at the Flyin' Spur was a stinkin' business, but you just have to show your muscle to Tamblyn's kind before they show you theirs! You can't deal peaceable with 'em. My old man tried to, he had his share of fightin' in the war, but they made him grab for his gun in the finish – an' they damn near sawed him in half with bullets!'

'What do you figure the play you made against Tamblyn in his own ranch yard'll result in, Mead?' asked Seth Diffin.

'It seems to have scared some of his riders, anyway,' the gunfighter answered. 'Maybe it'll dampen the ardour of the rest of his outfit – on the other hand, Tamblyn might make a fight right soon. I wanted to talk to you about that. If the Flyin' Spur makes an attack on any of the homesteads, we'll have to stick together an' fight together. Rifle shots'll carry far along this ridge. On your way home, Seth, make a detour around to Quillan's place. Tell Quillan to fire two shots in quick succession at the first sign of any trouble an' the rest of the nesters will come runnin'; if he hears two shots, he'll have to go damn quick in the direction they came from. That goes for all of us; we must stick together. If we see any of the Flying Spur riders comin', we fire two rifle shots as a warning; if we hear two warning shots, we run to help whoever's bein' attacked. I'll ride along the other side of the ridge later an' tell Hannaway of the arrangement.'

So it was that Mead Conant rode to the furthermost end of the ridge later that night. Gerry Hannaway and his sons were prepared to fight and fully agreed to the warning system.

Throughout the ride to the old soldier's homestead and on the return journey, Conant was acutely conscious of tha strange wound he had suffered somewhere deep inside from the biting words of the tearful Mildred Apsley.

She'd called him a killer; told him he was no better than the gun-hung gentry Tamblyn had gathered around him. He thought of the red hatred for Tamblyn and his outfit that had blazed inside him ever since that bullet-bitten night on Moroni Creek twelve years before. He remembered those gunfights of the intervening years: when it had been kill or be killed in the flash and blast of bucking six-guns. He remembered the way every tension-grinning outlaw face seemed to take on the appearance of Arch Tamblyn's features in the misty swirls of gunsmoke. Always, he had known through some mysterious agency, that he would survive the bullet-whining chaos of the moment to face Arch Tamblyn in person.

He knew it now and the red hatred inside him burned with stronger fire.

Maybe the girl was right.

Maybe he was just a killer and nothing more.

Five

If ever the hand of fate lay heavily upon the land of the Spanish Saddle range, it did so that night – the night of Seth Diffin's visit to the Apsley homestead.

Arch Tamblyn sat for a long time before the empty fieldstone fireplace in his ranch-house sucking on an equally empty pipe. Then he rose and made his way across the yard to the bunkhouse where the Flying Spur riders were making ready to turn in for the night. He booted the door open savagely and strode into the ranch crew's sleeping quarters.

Cowhands were standing about or sitting on their bunks. There was an air of numbness about them – it had held them since Mead Conant rode into the outfit's yard and had intensified with the quitting of such old trigger hands as Kersands, Wilkes, Heldkopf and Millick. Tamblyn glowered at the men in the yellow lamplight, his longhorn moustache bristling.

'If anyone else wants to quit, he can go now,' he rasped. 'Those who stay are gettin' gun-money from this moment on – three times what you're gettin' for ridin' range. From now on, it's war against Conant an'

those blasted nesters. In a couple of days I'll be usin'
those homesteads on North Ridge as line camps an'
Flying Spur cows'll be grazin' where the nesters
raised their crops. Anybody who hasn't the belly to see
it through can quit now!'

He contemplated the cow-wranglers with icy eyes.
That stirring of fear deep in his guts was not entirely
dispelled; it came back, in fact, with renewed force in
its quivering lest these hands should fail to be drawn
by his offer of big money, quit *en bloc* and leave him
alone against Conant. Outwardly, however, he main-
tained his tough, unwavering demeanour.

'Conant's some *hombre* to buck against,' declared
one of the riders cautiously.

'If that means you're scared of Conant an' you want
to pull out, pack yore warsack an' fork yore cayuse,'
rapped the rancher.

The cowboy sat slowly down upon his bunk. At his
obvious intention of staying some of the uncertainty
was taken from the eyes of the remaining occupants of
the bunkhouse.

'I didn't say I was quittin',' the man said. He forced
a weak grin. 'I didn't say I was scared, either – I ain't
scared of one man!' His ill-maintained grin belied his
words. He was scared to show his real feelings before
his range-companions and they were equally scared to
show theirs before Tamblyn and each other.

On the face of it, they were all staying.

'Good,' grunted Arch Tamblyn. 'This little ruckus
will be over in a couple of days, I promise you. It's gun-
money for you from here on.'

Tamblyn turned and strode from the bunkhouse.

Secretly, he was not sure of the loyalty of his riders. Conant had thrown a mighty big scare into the Flying Spur that afternoon; any one of the hands in the bunkhouse might decamp in the stillness of the night. Suppose they all sneaked away and left him to face Conant alone?

That quirk of fear started in his innards again.

But the hand of fate was upon the Spanish Saddle range that night and, from between the fingers of the hand of fate. two men came riding. They were tall and they rode in the white moonlight like mounted ghosts.

They came into the yard of the Flying Spur when the owner of that ranch was mid-way between the bunkhouse and his living-quarters. He heard the jingle of their saddle trappings as they came and he twisted around to face the newcomers, standing spread-legged in the dust of the yard.

The two riders came towards him and yanked reins to pull their travel-dusty broncs to a halt. The moon painted their long bodies with a stark whiteness.

Under the wide brims of their big sombreros, their lean faces were remarkably alike: thin, long-nosed, each with a slit of a mouth, each with lank staggles of black hair flopping over his proud-veined, skull-like forehead. Bitter lines, deep-etched like wind-scorings in desert rocks, were creased down their gaunt features. They sat their saddles with the bow-backed indolence of the desert rider, watching the rancher with cold, curiously flat eyes.

'You Tamblyn?' asked one. His voice was gritty and had a Texas drawl.

Tamblyn was taking in the Colt .45s the strangers

wore – two each, worn low and thonged down against their scrubby jeans.

'Yeah, I'm Tamblyn,' the rancher said.

The one who spoke first pulled the corners of his lips up to show stained teeth in something resembling a smile. He nodded his big-hatted head towards the rider at his side.

'Him an' me,' he announced, 'we're the Banselling brothers – Luther an' Brett.' The smile persisted, cold and without humour. The second rider merely watched Tamblyn with his hard eyes.

'The Bansellings, I've heard of you,' Tamblyn answered.

'Sure, you've heard of us. The Bansellings from the Texas Panhandle,' smiled the brother who did the talking.

'There was three of you,' said Tamblyn.

The thin smile disappeared.

'There used to be three of us – didn't there, Luther?'

'Yeah,' growled his brother.

'The third one was called Ace,' jerked Brett Banselling. 'He was killed in a ruckus back in Colorado – killed by an *hombre* name of Mead Conant.' He pronounced the name slowly and with deliberation. 'He shot Luther an' me up some, but Ace was the one he wanted an' Ace was the one he killed. We done got over our wounds now an' it'd be better for Conant if he'd killed us back in Colorado, 'cause we aim to kill him – don't we, Luther?'

'Yeah,' responded the taciturn Luther.

Brett Banselling hoisted his long body over the saddle and leaned down towards the owner of the

Flying Spur in a confidential manner. He jerked his thumb in a northerly direction.

'Back yonder, we heard tell Conant was in this country. We heard it from some fellers that were runnin' from here. They said they used to ride for you; they told us Conant did some hell-raisin' around here an' they weren't stayin' any longer. We figured there might be a place for us here on your spread.' Brett Banselling licked his thin lips as he finished speaking.

Arch Tamblyn stood in the moonlight watching the stark figures of the newcomers on their pawing mounts. He felt something warm rise up in him, quelling the quirk of fear at his stomach. That approximation of a smile that had spread across his windburned face when Cliff Dignan first brought news of Conant's return to the territory took possession of his features once more.

'Texas men!' he grated. 'My kind of men.' He tilted his head meaningly in the general direction of Brett Banselling's tied-down guns. 'Sure, there's a place for you on this outfit. Glad to have you around. I figure you boys are a right good swap for those blamed yellow-bellies that ran out on me. Take your cayuses into the barn an' come into the bunkhouse.'

The gun-hung Texans did so. They jingled their spurs into the sleeping quarters of the Flying Spur hands, their arrival causing the majority of the cowboys, now in their bunks, to jerk bolt upright and contemplate the jackal-lean gunmen with shrewd eyes.

Arch Tamblyn followed them in with the air of a master of ceremonies.

'Boys, these here are Brett an' Luther Banselling – they're joining up with the outfit.'

In the dim lamp-light, eyes widened and fixed on the gun-gear worn by the Texans with the flamboyance of slick-trigger men. Luther, the taciturn one, slanted his long frame against a bunk-post, cuffed back his dust-peppered sombrero and hooked his thumbs into the cartridge studded belt buckled against his flat belly.

'Where's Conant at?' he asked, directing the question at the owner of the Flying Spur.

'Somewhere up on a place called North Ridge. He's in with a bunch of homesteaders up there, but I don't know which ones: there are four families on the ridge. I aim to run the nesters off the ridge. Conant came into my yard today, shot two of my men an' said I wouldn't he runnin' anybody off anywhere.'

'So he's backin' the homesteaders,' grunted Brett Banselling. 'He's put himself up as their fightin' man, eh? Me an' Luther, we don't like nesters either: bein' from Texas we love 'em like we love stinkin' barbed wire fences – don't we, Luther?'

'Yeah.'

Brett Banselling fixed the rancher with his narrow eyes. He asked slowly: 'You got any plans made for takin' Conant an' the homesteaders?'

'Plans?' queried Tamblyn. 'No, we have no plans made.'

'Can't take Conant without a plan – he's too damned quick. Got to lay a plan an' catch his kind on the hop. That's what me an' Luther aim to do, get him caught in a plan an' smoke him down!'

'He means a gun-trap,' explained Luther with a bleak grin. 'Get him trapped an' cut in half by bullets before he knows what hit him is the only way you can deal with an *hombre* like Conant!'

'Which nester place is nearest the ranch — which can you hit at first?' Brett wanted to know.

'One owned by a young feller name of Carl Quillan; we can reach his place in less than an hour of ridin',' Tamblyn answered.

'Is he a fightin' man?' asked Brett.

'Naw. Anything but a fightin' man.'

'Um,' snorted the more talkative of the Banselling brothers. 'You got anybody who can go to North Ridge quiet-like an' find out just where Conant is campin' down?'

Tamblyn, with the distinct impression that his authority over the Flying Spur was being taken out of his hands, thought about that for a while.

'Yeah,' he stated at length. 'There's one galoot I can send out. An old *hombre* from Huajillo — if he does what I want properly, I'll give him a bottle of rye. He'd sell his soul for liquor an' I went a fair way to buyin' it long ago.'

Six

Throughout breakfast at the Apsley homestead on the morning following Mildred's outburst against Conant, the gunfighter was conscious of the girl bestowing bitter glances upon him. He ate moodily, wondering whether he could detect hatred in those glances.

There was a bitterness equal to that of Mildred in him. For the first time in a long period of time, he considered himself objectively. He wondered whether the girl was right. Perhaps he was simply a killer, despite the veneer of the law enforcement officer that covered his killings. Maybe something got into him that night on Moroni Creek that twisted him into a man-killer. He killed on the side of the law, sure, but maybe he was basically a man-killer – maybe all lawmen got that way eventually. It was a short step over a narrow line from killing to uphold the law to killing to break the law.

He ate his breakfast thinking of the lawmen who wound up with spotty reputations: Hickok's name was mud on a lot of tongues, so was Wes Hardin's, though there were damn few who had guts enough to tell Wes so to his face. There was an ugly pall, not to mention an Arizona murder warrant, hanging over the head of Wyatt Earp, recently marshal of Tombstone. who had hit a smart lick over the Colorado line. Maybe they all got that way in time. Maybe they got to thinking they were some kind of superior being because they could yank the snout of a six-gun out of leather faster than most. Maybe he was heading down the same trail to infamy, for all his fine ideas.

With the meal finished, Conant and Apsley strode outside the homestead. Apsley was visibly disturbed about his sister's attitude to the guest under their roof. He stood outside the shack in the bright sunshine of the morning, stuffing tobacco into his corn-cob pipe.

'I wouldn't take too much notice of Mildred, Mead. You know how it is with a woman, they don't see things the same way as a man.'

Conant fished in his shirt-pocket for the makings and stood watching a spiral of grey dust rising on the ridge-trail. It floated up over the sun-touched tops of an aspen-stand down the slope of the ridge-side some three hundred yards from the homestead.

The gunfighter moistened his newly-rolled smoke, still keeping his eyes on the plume of dust.

'Maybe they see some things the correct way, Dave,' he replied slowly. 'More correct than we give 'em credit for sometimes.' Then, with scarcely a change of intonation in his voice: 'There's a rider comin' up the ridge.'

Both stood stock still regarding the haze of dust and each was conscious of a strange apprehension. The rider came out of the aspens into full view on the ochre banner of the upward-winding trail.

Distance-dimmed as yet, he was a small man in range garb and a black hat. His mount was a pinto which looked as if it had seen better days and known better feed-boxes than the one where it currently found its fodder.

Something metallic glittered on the riding man's dark-toned vest.

'Sheriff Tyzack, of Huajillo,' mused Dave Apsely. 'What's he want up here?'

'Tyzack!' exclaimed Conant as the name struck a chord of memory. 'I know that name – seems I remember it from when I was a kid.'

'Sure,' Apsley answered. 'Time was when Andy Tyzack had a homestead up the side of Moroni Creek – somewhere beyond your old man's place. It was a long time ago – before we came to these parts.'

Conant smoked in silence for a while, absorbing this information and watching the rider grow bigger on the ridge-trail.

'I remember,' he began at length. 'He was the nearest thing we had to a neighbour, had a weakness for the bottle, too. How did he get to be law officer in Huajillo?'

Apsley spat into the red, dry dust.

'He's Tamblyn's man. Tamblyn runs Huajillo, as you know. When they got this region organized into a county, they made Huajillo the seat an' Tamblyn pushed Tyzack for the office of Sheriff. They say Tamblyn has the local politics in his pocket to the extent that he has the county pay Tyzack in bottles of cheap liquor, instead of dollars.'

The riding man came closer, a slight figure sagging in the saddle with a weary warp to its shoulders. He had a scrubby beard and an unkempt moustache; his eyes were redrimmed and watery and his nose was the label on a two-legged whiskey bottle. Tyzack wore a Peacemaker Colt holster high at his waist and the star on his buckskin vest was highly incongruous.

Conant watched him ride up to the homestead and hoist the pinto to a halt. The gunfighter regarded the newcomer with more pity than he knew was in him. He remembered the face of Tyzack from when he was a kid. It was more lined, now; lined with the deep, bitter etching of disillusion.

Andy Tyzack sat slumped in the saddle looking at Conant almost apologetically.

'You Mead Conant?' he asked. His voice was thin, little more than the whine of a man who had been kicked down so many times he was no longer interested in trying to pull himself up. He answered his own question: 'Yeah, I can see you are – I remember you from when you were a kid.'

'I remember you, too, Sheriff, an' the homestead you had on Moroni Creek,' Conant stated coldly.

The mounted man studied the ground around the forefeet of his pinto, then tugged awkwardly at his straggly moustache. Conant pushed the point: 'Did you quit bein' a homesteader after what happened at my old man's place?'

Tyzack said gruffly:

'Mister Tamblyn bought me out.'

Mead Conant's eyebrows arched up.

'*Mister* Tamblyn,' he repeated, '*bought you out!*'

The law officer continued to study the dusty ground, avoiding the eyes of the tall, gun-hung man standing at the homesteader's side. Conant noted how Tyzack's eyes glided clear of his own. Nevertheless, the watery eyes of the sheriff transferred their gaze from the ground to take in the homestead. They came to rest on the small barn in which Conant's bronc was standing with Apsley's animal. Conant did not fail to notice Tyzack's interest in the barn.

The gunfighter stood close to his host, the thumbs of his bronze hands caught into his gunbelt close to the buckle. What had Tyzack meant by saying the owner of the Flying Spur had bought out his homestead? Dimly, from the past that lay beyond that bullet-broken night when his father and brothers died on Moroni Creek, he recalled an incident. He remembered Arch Tamblyn himself, with gun-flourishing riders reined up at his back and smiling tight-lipped smirks. He remembered Tamblyn offering to 'buy' his father's homestead claim for a sum that was an insult. He remembered his father standing in the door of the cabin, telling Tamblyn to go to hell in his slow Southern drawl. He recalled Tamblyn's grating voice informing his father that he and his men would return to buy the place with bullets. In a couple of weeks, when the moon was dark, they came.

Conant saw the same pattern re-enacted at Andy Tyzack's place.

'So they came an' bought you out for a price that would hardly buy a week's makings,' observed the gunfighter with bitterness.

'In his case, they say, it was the price of a half-bottle

of rotgut,' Dave Apsley stated, a strange hardness in his voice.

Tyzack was contemplating the ground once more.

'Can't say I blame you,' Conant added. 'You couldn't hope to fight 'em alone – if fightin' ever entered yore head. You saw what they did to my kin an' I guess that was lesson enough for you. What d'you want here?'

For the first time, Andy Tyzack regarded the gunfighter squarely.

'I want you,' he declared in his wheezy whine. 'Mr Tamblyn was in town this mornin'. He told me about you killin' three men, Spade Lacy, Cliff Dignan an' Schneeman – you're wanted for murder, Conant.' Tyzack spoke as if this was a fact belonging to another world and scarcely touching his. There was no conviction in his voice when he added: 'I came out to get you.'

Conant shook his head in a slow negative.

'You couldn't take me in, Andy. You and twenty more like you couldn't do it an' you know it damned well. Go back an' tell Arch Tamblyn to come an' get me, then get yoreself propped up against a bar in Huajillo, where you belong.'

Andy Tyzack's eyes appeared to grow even more watery. He sat still in his saddle for a long instant, then he spread his hands in a gesture of disinterest. Without a word, he pranced his lean pinto around and took it off along the ridge-trail in the direction from which he came. Dust hazed in his back-trail as he rode away. The weary warp of his shoulders was increased.

Mildred Apsley had been standing at the door of the cabin since shortly after Tyzack's arrival. She moved across to the two men, stood at their backs and watched the departing rider dwindle down the ridge side.

'That poor old man,' she said softly. 'I always feel sorry for him. He must have known you'd never give yourself up to him' – there was a hardness in this last sentence which was directed at Conant.

'He's a dirty little runny,' her brother snorted. 'He knew he didn't have a hope of takin' Mead in before ever he rode out here. See the way he just turned around an' rode?'

Conant stood in silence watching Andy Tyzack disappear into the thick of the aspen stand. Curiously, like Mildred, he felt sorry for the sheriff, too. He remembered the way Tyzack's watery eyes had roved the homestead, paying particular attention to his horse alongside Apsley's in the barn.

'He didn't come out here to take me in, that was just talk,' he remarked levelly. 'He came out here to have a look-see and find out where I was beddin' down. He saw my horse in your barn without its saddle an' he knows I'm spendin' my nights here. He was sent here to find out what part of the ridge I'm holin' up on. Tamblyn sent him, for sure.'

'That talk he made about wantin' you for murder – d'you think there's a warrant out for you?' asked Apsley.

'Sure there's a warrant out. Those killin's were self-defence, but Tyzack is Tamblyn's man an' he's the lawful County Sheriff, after all. He can put a murder warrant out for me, an' the Flyin' Spur bunch can gun me down if they catch me nappin' an' swear out their tongues that I was wanted for murder an' died resistin' arrest. There's trouble blowin' up an' I have a hunch it'll split wide open before long.'

Conant turned his head slightly and saw Mildred's gently-moulded face looking at his in a frank and unguarded instant. He saw something in her wide and intelligent eyes that caused a warm surge to rise in him. Despite the hardness of her tone when she last addressed him, he saw fear in her eyes – not fear *of* him, but fear *for* him.

Strangely, a ragged banner of grey cloud, alone in an otherwise clear azure sky, floated across the face of the bright sun and cast the homestead and the trio into a full minute of shadow.

Somehow, it seemed to be an omen.

Andy Tyzack allowed his pinto to take its own pace down the ridge side and over the sun-washed, scrub-dotted flats that eventually gave way to coarse-grass rangeland where longhorns bearing the Flying Spur iron browsed.

The Sheriff of Huajillo County rode with a bitter regret starting somewhere in his soul. Things he had tried to close his eyes to for many years past persisted in floating to the top of his consciousness and staying there to rankle. For the first time in he knew not how long, he looked at himself objectively, weighed what he set out to be against what he had become. The sum total failed to impress him.

Nevertheless, he turned his pinto in at the arched gateway of the Flying Spur yard, thinking as he did so that he was like a dog returning home to its master.

He found Tamblyn in the living-room of the ranch-house. The gun-hung brothers Banselling lounged in chairs, each stretching his lean legs with spurred, high-heeled boots crossed. Tamblyn whirled around from the window from where he had been contemplating the distant straggle of the Dragoon mountains.

'Well?' he demanded with eagerness. 'Did you see him? Did you find out where he's holin' up?'

Tyzack licked his moustache-fringed lip nervously.

'Yeah. Apsley's place,' he husked.

'Apsley's place!' exclaimed the rancher. 'You sure he was stayin' there, not just visitin'?'

'His bronc was in the stable without a saddle, been there all night obviously,' Tyzack said wearily.

Arch Tamblyn smirked.

'Did you tell him you wanted him for those killin's?'

'Yeah. He told me I couldn't take him an' I knew it, so I turned my cayuse around an' came back.'

'He didn't make any gunplay?'

'He made no attempt – just told me to ride back to town an' have a drink.'

A dry chuckle started in Tamblyn's throat and increased to a laugh that shook his paunch. From their seats, the brothers Banselling regarded him with cold eyes.

'You did pretty well, Andy,' praised Tamblyn, 'an' Conant has technically resisted arrest. Killers that resist arrest frequently get gunned down, don't they, boys?'

The Banselling brothers quirked up the corners of their slitted mouths as if the muscles of each gaunt, beard-bristled face were activated by a single string.

Tamblyn caught up a sheet of paper from a small

table nearby and reached for a stub of pencil. He drew a large cucumber-shape on the paper.

'North Ridge,' he announced, showing the diagram to the Texas trigger-slicks. The rancher laid the paper on the table and the Texans stood up and joined him.

Tamblyn drew a cross at the eastern end of his diagram.

'That's Apsley's homestead, where this Conant is campin' down,' he explained. He placed another cross some distance west along the ridge.

'Diffin's – owned by two brothers.'

His next indication was placed even further to the west, but more to the north than any of the previous crosses. In slow and deliberate tones, Arch Tamblyn said: 'That's Quillan's, the nearest nester-roost to the Flyin' Spur.' His final cross was placed at the most isolated westerly flank of the ridge.

'That's the last of the bunch, owned by a damned Yankee, name of Hannaway,' the rancher grated bitterly. He stabbed a horny finger at the cross marking the Quillan holding. Set in their sun-, wind-, and age-etched creases, his eyes were glittering savagely.

'We can be at Quillan's an' shoot the place up in no time at all,' he stated. 'Conant, over here at Apsley's place, will come runnin' like a hungry wrangler hearin' the cook call just as soon as he hears the shootin'.'

'An'?' asked Brett Banselling.

'An' here,' continued Tamblyn, thumbing an area between the cross marking the Apsley holding and that indicating the Quillan homestead, 'the trail winds into a deep gully where there's cover a-plenty –

aspens, oak, poinsietta an' big, high rocks. It's narrow, too, an' the only possible way Conant can reach the Quillan place.'

Brett Banselling's eyes flashed.

'Sounds like a man could lay there, don't it, Luther.'

'Yeah,' agreed Luther.

'Take some of the other boys with you,' suggested Tamblyn. 'Conant is hell with his gun – the last two guys who laid for him came off second best.'

'We know he's hell with his gun,' rapped Brett. 'We caught his slugs once, but that won't happen again. We're carryin' our guns for Ace in this an' it won't be us who come off second best – eh, Luther?'

'Naw,' scowled Luther.

For an instant the Texas gun-slingers stood contemplating the diagram with tough, humourless grins on their faces.

Over by the door, Andy Tyzack shuffled his feet. Arch Tamblyn glowered at him as if realizing that the sheriff was still in the room.

'What the hell're you hangin' around for, Andy?' he snorted. 'Sashay back to town!'

'I was just goin',' mumbled Tyzack. He turned and shuffled for the yard. Even the ring of his spurs lacked spirit.

Tyzack untied his reins from the hitch-rack in the yard, climbed into the saddle and took the pinto off the Flying Spur headquarters at a slow walk. Memories had a disturbing way of coming back to him when he was cold sober, as he was now, and he couldn't shut them out today. He realized dimly that it was the sight of the kid from Moroni Creek who had returned as a

gun-heavy fighting man that had set the disturbing
memories into action. Despite what Andy Tyzack had
become with the years, little more than a hound-dog at
Arch Tamblyn's heel, he knew that Mead Conant and
the nester families on North Ridge were his kind of
people.

He rode to Huajillo thinking of the gun-trap he had
heard arranged at the Flying Spur headquarters – the
beginning of a plot to massacre his kind of people. He
remembered the night he crouched behind a locked
cabin door on Moroni Creek twelve years before. He
was full of whiskey but that did not dispel his quaking
fear. He could hear the hard blasting of killers' guns
and the high-licking flames from the blazing cabin
along the creek flared over the tops of the dark trees
and he knew the Flying Spur gunhands might visit
his homestead next.

They came the following day, smiling jackal smiles
and with their hands playing close to the curving
butts of the six-guns at their thighs. They offered
Tyzack an insulting price for the little holding he had
tried to shape into a small farm. The meaningful tilt of
their sombrero brims in the general direction of the
still smouldering ruins of the Conant homestead indi-
cated the consequences of a refusal.

Tyzack accepted and became clay in the hands of
the owner of the Flying Spur.

He reflected on his full cup of bitterness until he
was close to the straggling town of Huajillo. He
entered the single street, with its weather-warped
wooden frontages, as the sun reached its mid-day
apex. There was a squareness to the set of his shoul-

ders that they had not held for years and he surprised a number of loafers by riding clear past the Desert Star saloon without even looking at its peeled facade and heading straight for his office.

Seven

The threat of impending trouble lingered long over the Apsley homestead.

At noon, Mead Conant stepped out of the cabin and eyed the sky as if what he feared might be seen as a physical thing up there in the sparse flecks of cloud on the sun-washed vastness of the wide blue. Since that morning he had been aware of a less stiff attitude towards him on the part of Mildred Apsley. The open hostility of the previous night when he found her in tears by the small barn was replaced by a guarded politeness, as if the girl were ashamed of her tears and what she had said. It was a restrained friendship, however, with nothing in it of the open friendliness she had shown when her brother first brought him to the holding.

Conant was sorry her attitude towards him had this cautious quality. He liked the nester girl with her spun-gold hair and her wide, frank eyes. She forced herself into his thoughts time and again and he tried in vain to exclude her from them.

This was no time to think of women – think of their safety if what he sensed was blowing up blew wide

71

open, yes, but to think of them in any other way was idle and foolish. It was a time to think of quick defensive action and how best you could defend your life against the fellow over the hump who was coming to try to take it.

And there was a fellow – a whole bunch of fellows – coming over the hump, Conant knew. He seemed to sense it strongly now and that morning's visit of Andy Tyzack, who came on a weak pretence to size up the situation with a watery eye, bore out his premonition. There was bound to be some kind of retaliation for what he had done at the Flying Spur headquarters or that Texas hellion, Arch Tamblyn, had grown too old and had lost his guts as had the riders who packed their warsacks and rode out after the tempestuous visit of Conant with the remains of Spade Lacy draped over his saddle. This was unlikely; Conant knew that. Retaliation would come soon. It would come to North Ridge and maybe its coming was Mead Conant's doing. Perhaps he was just a killer, as the tearful girl said. Perhaps his spectacular action at the Flying Spur the previous day would bring death to roost on North Ridge where, otherwise, it might not settle.

There was death in the air; he felt it on the hot breeze that blew up from the flats below the ridge.

He could see a long way down the ridge side to where the land flattened away to scrub spattered distances which in turn became grassland where tiny moving dots denoted grazing Flying Spur stock. It was good land, Conant thought. Not so good as the shortgrass ranges up to the north, sure, but good land for the rangy Texas longhorns the Flying Spur wrangled.

The Spanish Saddle rangeland would give Tamblyn's stock a heaviness of flesh which would bring good prices in the St Louis markets. Many another man would be well satisfied with what Tamblyn already owned, the gunfighter mused. But not Arch Tamblyn. He came into Arizona Territory early and he grabbed himself a sizeable piece and here he was – still grabbing. He would continue grabbing so long as he had strength and man-power enough to do so. You had to stand up against his kind – stand up and fight like all hell.

You just had to if you were any kind of man at all.

Hoof-clatter and clink of harness-trappings at his back caused Mead Conant to whirl about with the stealthy, cat-footed swiftness of a reputation-owning gunslick.

He saw three riders coming down the trail which snaked westerly along the ridge from the Apsley homestead. He recognized the mounted trio: the Diffin brothers and lean, Lincolnesque Gerry Hannaway, and his tensed hands fell away from the proximity of his twin guns.

Even at this distance of several hundred yards, something about the attitude of the riders registered on Conant; something approaching disillusion and even despair.

He stood straddle-legged, still in that gunfighter's attitude into which he had danced, watching them draw nearer to the cabin. Dave Apsley must have seen them from the window for he came out of the building and joined Conant.

Without speaking, they watched the horsemen ride

up and yank their animals to a halt. Tall Gerry Hannaway was to the fore, long, lean Seth and his shorter brother Bill sat their saddles a little behind Hannaway. Three sun-coloured faces grave and unsmiling.

There was no greeting, Hannaway simply said, curtly:

'Quillan's pullin' out.'

'No!' exploded Dave Apsley. 'He can't be!'

'He is,' replied Bill Diffin flatly. 'Gerry here decided he'd ride along the ridge just to see if everythin' was all right with everyone. He reached Quillan's place an' found Carl and Becky packin'. Quillan said he was scared that what you did at the Flyin' Spur would loose all hell on the ridge an' he wasn't layin' his wife an' baby wide open to that. Then Gerry saw it wasn't no use arguin' so he came along the ridge to our place. We all decided to come down here an' tell you.'

Conant contemplated the serious-cast faces of the mounted men. They were tough and resolute, willing to fight and die for what they owned, but the effect on their morale of one of their neighbours running before the threat of impending trouble was plain to see. Conant felt a cold disgust rise within him. Quillan must have spent months whipping his holding into the neat little farm it was now, but here he was, shying away from the place he had carved for his family like a scared steer running from a bellowing rider and setting the seeds of panic flourishing among his neighbours.

Conant knew the viewpoints of both sides of the homestead wrangles – the nester side and the cowman side. Faced with seeing Carl Quillan run from his holding, he thought that maybe the cattlemen's view was the right one after all: nesters were scared rabbits who grubbed in the dirt and ruined good beef pasture. He spat into the dust with sudden disgust at his own thought. He was a nester kid himself once and his kin were, nesters who had guts enough to stand and fight for their claims – even as these men now before him would have guts enough for the fight.

'Quillan can't do it,' he grated. 'If he wants to call himself a man, he'll have to stand by his neighbours an' fight for his home – he owes it to himself an' his family an' to you all. I'll ride over an' try talkin' him into stayin'. I can't see a man throw his self-respect an' his months of hard work into the wind that way.'

'Yeah,' agreed Dave Apsley. 'I'll come with you – we'll all go.' He hastened to the barn to saddle the horses.

Mildred appeared in the doorway of the cabin and came walking towards the mounted visitors. They tipped their hats and mumbled their 'good days'. The girl assessed their grave expressions and read the trouble in their faces.

'What's the matter?' she asked.

Mead Conant supplied the answer: 'Carl Quillan's pulling up his stakes an' runnin'.'

Mildred gasped.

'Oh. no! He can't just run away and leave it all – he's worked so hard on his homestead and Becky was so proud of their little home. It was the only home they ever had. Where will they go?'

'Carl said he figured he could get a job in Tucson

when I spoke to him,' said Gerry Hannaway.

'Tucson!' The girl said it almost with disgust. 'Tucson's growing, it's getting to be a big town; one day it'll be a city like Chicago or St Louis. Carl and Becky will become just another pair of town-dwellers, living on a street instead of having a place of their own out in the clean air!'

Conant felt admiration for the girl. He hadn't thought along those lines; such thought probably came from the girl's own experience in a city school. He turned and walked towards the barn to help Dave with the mounts.

Bill Diffin said: 'You're right, Mildred. If the Quillans run they'll throw away their chance to live free as a bird an' throw their self-respect an' work into the wind, as Mead says.'

'He said that?' asked the girl musingly, as if the repeated remark of Conant's revealed some facet of his character otherwise hidden from her.

Conant and Apsley came walking their animals over from the barn, swung into their saddles, joined the trio of nesters and the knot of mounted men moved off up the ridge trail.

In the neat yard of the Quillan homestead, the buggy load of furniture was a silent but eloquent admission of defeat. Quillan was in the act of hefting a chair atop the pile when the five riders came into his holding. His pretty young wife was standing by the door of the homestead contemplating a red rambler-rose which climbed on green tendrils up a porch stanchion. Conant did not miss the significance of that. The rose was a woman's touch. Probably Becky

Quillan planted it and cared for it – and now she was leaving it.

There was something almost hostile in Carl Quillan's attitude as he turned to face the newcomers after settling the chair into the rest of the piled furnishings. Conant paced his bronc to the front of the group and yanked his rein.

'So you're pullin' out, Carl,' he said in a colourless tone.

'Yeah. I'm pullin' out before I get gunned out. I have a wife an' kids an' we all have plenty to live for!' The young nester grew red in the face. 'I don't want what happened to your family down on Moroni Creek years ago to happen to mine!'

'That's understandable,' Conant answered. 'I hear you're figurin' on goin' to Tucson.'

'Yeah. I can get a job in Tucson an' live in peace without wakin' up nights an' wonderin' if Tamblyn's hellions are ridin' down on my home. I can get work easily enough. I have a tolerable education; I can work as a clerk, or I can work with my hands.'

Conant gave the neat little homestead a sweeping glance.

'I know you can work, Carl, this homestead proves it – it's a credit to you. That's why it's a plumb pity to run off an' leave it.'

Quillan studied the ground for a while.

'I can't stay,' he mumbled. 'It's not so much me as Becky an' the kids.'

Conant called across to the dark-haired girl on the porch.

'How do you feel about leavin' your home an'

runnin' away, Miz' Quillan?'

Veins of sunlight angled across the porch and touched highlights to the peaked but pretty features of Becky Quillan.

'I don't want to go, naturally,' she answered slowly. 'Carl has worked so hard to build the homestead and I love living out here, but we're frightened, Mr Conant, frightened for the children and ourselves.'

Conant addressed both Quillan and his wife: 'Listen, last time I was here I told you the Flyin' Spur gunnies wouldn't do to your family what they did to mine – I promised you that. Stand by your home an' neighbours an' I'll gun down any range-scum who try to run you off. I don't boast about it, but my reputation's big. Think about it: your self-respect, your hard work, a place of your own for the wife an' kids – it's all at stake!'

Conant waved his hand to indicate the horsemen at his back.

'All your neighbours are with you, you can be sure of that,' he added.

There was a brief silence, then, from the porch, Becky Quillan said: 'Maybe we should stay, Carl. Maybe it's just cowardice to run.' Her slender hand reached out and fondled the climbing rose with a strangely significant gesture.

Perhaps her use of the word 'cowardice' did it. Quillan squared his shoulders and set his mouth into a tight line.

'All right,' he said with determination. 'All right! We'll stay!'

Eight

That afternoon, Andy Tyzack sat in his grubby little office with his feet on the spur-scarred desk. He sat there a long time, thinking about what he had heard at the Flying Spur ranch-house. Those hissed words that passed between Arch Tamblyn and the brothers Banselling.

A gun trap for Conant. That night.

An attack on the Quillan homestead that would bring Conant running; running into a gun-trap in the deep gully through which the trail to the Quillan place passed. The Banselling brothers would be there, somewhere in the aspens and rocks – waiting to even up for Ace Banselling who fell before Mead Conant's gun in a wild ruckus somewhere in Colorado.

An echo of that quivering fear he had known the night the Flying Spur gutted the Conant homestead crept upwards in him. He had a sudden, stark vision of Carl Quillan and his family lying dead in a razed and smouldering homestead and Conant butchered in the aspens of the gully through which the ridge-trail snaked. His kind of people – nesters – killed by Tamblyn's quick-trigger riders.

Tyzack started to his feet suddenly and slammed his fist down on the dusty desk. He couldn't allow it!

Twelve years ago he had quaked in his cabin while Tamblyn's riders blazed their hot lead at the Conants. He had lived with the memory ever since, tried to wash it away in liquor, but whiskey only served to etch it deeper into his brain. He hadn't gone to the aid of the Conants that night twelve years ago; he could make up for it now by warning the Quillans and Mead Conant.

The Flying Spur men would choose the right time to make their play – in the still darkness of the evening; maybe he could reach North Ridge ahead of them and warn Conant of the intended raid on the Quillan place, meant as a device to lure him into a gun-trap.

Andy Tyzack took stock of himself. He'd been a worm under the rock for a long time, but now he was coming out, by cracky! Coming out against Arch Tamblyn who'd played master to his hound-dog for too long; coming out to fight for his kind of people.

There was a bottle three-quarters full of Crow whiskey standing in the gritty dust of the bureau by the grimy window. Tyzack snatched it up and took a stiff peg of the liquor, but not too much. He swallowed the liquor then hurled the bottle against the wall; shards of broken glass tinkled to the floor and the whiskey streamed down the wall to pool around them.

The peg he'd taken was for courage.

From now on, Andy Tyzack was off the bottle.

The late afternoon sunlight touched deep orange

fingers along the warped and flaked false-fronts of
Huajillo when Tyzack rode out. He saddled his pinto
in the alley at the rear of the law-office, rode out in the
opposite direction to North Ridge, using the alley and
an obscure back-trail to take him clear of the
cowtown.

On the desert fringe, he circled his mount and
headed for North Ridge on a trail that snaked through
the scrub and kept clear of the Flying Spur graze-
land. An hour of riding at a steady canter brought the
sheriff of Huajillo County within sight of the tree-
grown sweep of North Ridge. Had he not been deep in
thought and had his sight not been blurred by the
advance of age and the effects of long binges on neat
rotgut, he might have caught sight of the two horsemen along the trail, well ahead of him.

He did not see the pair of riders, but they saw him.
They were of the breed that frequently turned to scru-
tinise its backtrail, even on the most innocent of
horseback journeys. They turned, saw Tyzack's growing dust and went to ground in the thick scrub lining
the trail.

Andy Tyzack came up-trail. There was a sudden
flurry in the brush and two riders came rowelling
their horses out on to the trail to rein them up, sprad-
dle legged in the sheriff's path.

Two tall and lean riders, stitching back their face-
muscles in cold, bleak grins.

Brett and Luther Banselling.

Cold shock slammed itself through Tyzack's being
as he yanked leather to halt the pinto pony. There was
an evening haze already sifting down on the desert-

lands; the red-tinged light of the slow-dying sun lanced through it and touched a bloody glint to the trappings of the Banselling brothers and their horses, picking out the metal of the big Colts curving in their whanged-down holsters.

'Waal,' drawled Brett. It seemed a point of tradition that Brett always led off when the Texas brothers made talk. 'Waal, it's the sheriff, Luther – Sheriff Tyzack of Huajillo!'

Luther, still holding his cold grin, leaned forward in his saddle and crossed sun-darkened wrists over his pommel.

'Yeah,' he smirked. 'Funny he should ride for North Ridge just as we was goin' to take a look-see at that whereabouts our ownselves.' It was a flat and colourless comment. Tyzack sat rigid in the saddle staring at the gun-heavy pair from the Texas Panhandle.

His pinto danced back a couple of nervous steps in the dust of the trail and there was a sudden ominous chill to the edge of the slight desert wind.

'It's plumb funny, as you say, Luther,' Brett Banselling replied.

'Remember what Tamblyn said right after the sheriff here left? He said he didn't trust him around any nester trouble. Ain't it funny he should be headin' for North Ridge?'

There was a tension-strung moment of silence in which the two lean Texans smiled their wolfish smiles. They were cat-and-mousing Tyzack and he knew it.

Maybe they were trying to goad him into a clumsy claw for his gun. He was no gunhand and the years of rotgut booze had put a shake into his hand. He hadn't a Chinaman's chance of drawing his iron on these whipcord-lean Texas killers.

Luther screwed up his mouth into a small prune shape and spat into the dust.

'Tamblyn don't trust him around any nester trouble,' he declared in a grating drawl. 'Me, I don't trust him nohow. Can't help it. I got that way about anybody walkin' behind a tin-star a long time back!'

Very slowly, Luther Banselling's talon-like hands unfolded from the top of his saddle-horn and curved in towards his body.

'I got the same way about tin-stars my ownself,' answered his brother. Then he said in a hard voice: 'The gab-fest is over – we've finished talkin'!'

Tyzack didn't see the hands of Brett Banselling move for the holsters at his thighs, but they were, suddenly full of red-belching six-guns.

Luther's hands dipped and arced upwards a split second after his brother made his play, his twin Colts spitting out in a bellowing flash of red.

A quick blackness took hold of Andy Tyzack and gathered him into its womb. He hurtled back in the saddle, his head thrown back and his body stiffened. The pinto kicked its forelegs high. Tyzack's boots slithered out of the stirrups and he dropped backwards over the pinto's rump to flop limply into the trail-side brush.

The gunsmoke curled in a thick, grey-blue haze. Through it, Luther Banselling said: 'Yeah – we've finished talkin'.'

Brett yelled out a throaty whoop which set Tyzack's already scared pony to turning its tail and running away down-trail.

The Texas gun-hawks shoved their Colts into their holsters, yanked their horses' heads around and resumed their journey to North Ridge without bestowing another glance on the crumpled form sprawled in the brush.

The scent of Becky's climbing rose was strong and sweet in the nostrils of Carl Quillan as he stood on the homestead porch. Lamplight from the open doorway sprayed out in a yellow wash, throwing his shadow across the porch and the yard.

The moon was dimmed by swiftly moving clouds which had blown up that evening. In the darkened stands of trees along the ridge, a hoot-owl whooped his deep-noted call. Inside the cabin, the youngsters were asleep and Becky was settling the unloaded furniture into its old position. Another shadow joined Quillan's in the pool of lamplight and he smelt the sweetness of Becky's hair as she stood close to his back.

'I think you did the right thing in staying, Carl,' she said softly. 'After all the work you put into making this place out of nothing, I'll always think of it as being something very special.'

Quillan managed a wry smile.

'It is something special,' he answered. 'I didn't realize how special and how much it meant to me until I packed our trappin's on the buggy. I was only thinking of you an' the kids when I decided to pull out, though.'

'Of course you were,' she said, resting her hands gently on his shoulders. 'You're no coward—'

She broke off suddenly, tensing her slim body into

upright straightness, her face staring out into the cloud-shrouded night.

'Did you hear that, Carl?' Her voice was husked with an edge of fear.

'No. I heard nothing.'

'Listen!'

Growing louder in the darkness beyond the pool of lamplight came the unmistakable tramp of walking horses and the ring of harness trapping. Horses were coming along the ridge-trail towards the yard of the homestead. Quillan saw them and their riders come out of the blackness as a jogging cluster of wide-hatted shapes.

'It might be Conant an' some of the other home-steaders again,' he told his wife. But the statement carried no conviction for he knew there were too many approaching riders. 'Get into the house an' stay there,' he added with a panicky quiver in his voice.

Becky moved into the cabin. Quillan came after her, grabbed the gun-gear with a loaded Colt .38 which had hung on a peg close to the door ever since Tamblyn's riders came with the news that the nesters were to pull up their stakes before September first. He buckled the gear on and yanked the revolver from the holster. Under the peg, a Winchester was propped against the wall.

Quillan moved back to stand framed in the door. He held his gunhand around the back of his leg so the six-gun could not be seen.

The riders were bigger now and the tramp of their horses' hooves louder. They came into the yard in a deliberately moving bundle. Into the pooling lamplight they rode and their faces became yellow masks, tight and drawn with malignantly glinting eyes.

Arch Tamblyn himself was in the lead, his face like that of a man possessed by the devil. The shadow of his sombrero put a black half-moon on the upper part of his face, but his hard, cold eyes glittered evilly out of the darkness.

The Flying Spur riders reined up, forming a line fronting the homesteader dwelling.

Carl Quillan held a spraddle-legged pose in the door, still holding the Colt out of sight.

'What do you want?' he demanded in a voice that lacked firmness.

Tamblyn answered in a hard, grating voice, a flat voice devoid of any edge of emotion: 'You can thank yore gunslinging friend, Conant, for this, Quillan. After tonight, there ain't goin' to be any nesters on North Ridge, an' these homesteads'll be my line-camps.'

The rancher's knot-veined hands tightened on the Winchester he held canted across his saddle-horn. He raised the weapon slightly and, as if this was a signal for which they waited, the riders clustered about him fanned around the yard in a half circle, moving for their guns as they danced their mounts into sidelong movement.

Down the ridge, another hoot-owl whooped a brief and lonesome call.

Carl Quillan brought the Colt .38 up from behind his leg slowly.

'Don't start anythin', Tamblyn,' he stated. Already, he felt the fingers of doom clutching their cold grasp around his heart.

Arch Tamblyn began to laugh. The laugh started at his throat and it sounded like someone rattling a half-dozen pebbles in a rusty can. The hard-faced riders at the rancher's back took up the laugh in sympathy and the humourless chuckle rippled gratingly among them.

Tamblyn's chuckling ceased abruptly.

The Winchester in his grip came up to the firing position.

Quillan crouched and threw himself forward a split second before the rancher blasted an echo-shattering shot at him. Shards of wood splintered away from the doorpost as the slug slapped into it. Tamblyn's horse, startled by the shot, reared high, shaking its head in alarm. Carl Quillan hit the lamplit dust on his knees and triggered a panicky shot at the Flying Spur invaders. It went wide, whanging away into the sky.

The Flying Spur horses reared and jumped fractiously; gunsmoke banners hazed flatly over the yard.

Strangely distant, one of the children in the house began to cry.

Quillan knelt in the dust for an oddly detached moment, clutching the Colt, feeling the coarseness of the dust through the thin fabric of his jeans and quivering from head to toe.

The horses of the raiders danced in panic with a jingle of ringbits. Quillan saw rifles and six-guns coming up, saw his buggy standing a matter of yards away and started crawling for the cover of one of the iron-rimmed wheels.

A gun flashed out of the dark cluster of riders, the slug spurting up a spout of dust close to the nester's leg as he scooted on his knees for the underside of the buggy. He turned his head in the whirling dust and gunsmoke – and saw his wife coming out of the door of their home at a crouch, holding the Winchester and moving with a peculiar slow motion. Quillan heard his own voice yelling: 'No, Becky – go back!'

Things happened in a series of separate pictures. Becky fired the Winchester with a flash and slam. Arch Tamblyn dropped his carbine and clutched at his arm, shouting a stream of filthy language up to the dark sky. A blazing crackle of fire sprayed out of the midst of the mounted men. Becky stiffened and began to topple forward with her head thrown back limply.

Quillan was crawling madly for the scant shelter of the underside of the buggy, triggering the Colt into blazing, bucking life as he moved, shooting wildly and madly at the Flying Spur horsemen. A crimson haze swam before his eyes; through it, he saw the raiders as milling, half-formed shapes.

He did not hear the sound of the shots which killed him. The last of this world's noises to reach his ears were the cries of his children in the cabin.

It was like coming out of a deep sleep after being drunk on cheap liquor, but every last inch of his body ached, a couple of hot knives seemed to be stabbing into his chest and he could hear his own breath, wheezing and soughing deeply.

Something alive was muzzling wetly at his face.

Sheriff Andy Tyzack opened his eyes painfully.

Thoughts came swimming back in confused disorder: two chill-eyed Texas men; shots, half-heard; the notion of an unsuspecting rider being shot down in a gun-trap. He was sprawled in the brush, looking up at the dark sky. His scrubby little pinto, which had wandered back to its master after being hazed off by the Bansellings, was nuzzling at his face.

Tyzack began slowly to get his thoughts into order. He was still alive, in bad shape and pain-racked, but alive. There was a gun-trap being laid for Conant up on North Ridge and the Flying Spur intended running off the homesteaders with blazing guns. He had to do something about it.

It came to him that the bullet-carnage might be over, Conant and the nesters dead. Then, a distant but unmistakeable clatter of carbine-fire sounded thinly off North Ridge.

Tyzack moved experimentally in the dry roots of the brush. He still had control of his limbs, but it seemed as if the fires of hell were blazing inside his chest.

Maybe, if the pinto would hold still, he could hoist himself up the dangling rein and into the saddle. He'd try, by cracky!

Nine

In the reek of cordite smoke and the whirling, risen dust, Arch Tamblyn clutched the shoulder wounded by the shot from Becky Quillan's carbine. He yanked back his horse, cursing between clenched teeth.

In the lamplight which sprayed into the homestead yard from the windows and the open door of the nester dwelling, the woman lay flat, face first in the dust; her husband was coiled up in a still bundle close to the buggy.

From inside the house, the frenzied cries of the terrified children sounded continuously.

'Split up,' grated the owner of the Flying Spur. 'Half of you ride for that gully where the Bansellings are waitin' for Conant, the rest make for the Diffin place. Those damn Diffins are sure to come runnin' this way after hearin' our shots!'

'What about Hannaway, back along the ridge?' queried one of the riders.

'Forget him. We'll take him later. He's too isolated to bother us right now. First, I want to see Conant's wagon fixed for good an' all. C'mon!'

Holding his wounded shoulder, the old Texan spiked his spur-rowels into his horse's flanks, raking the animal into a quick lope eastward along the timbered ridge. His big-hatted riders went streaming after him like shadowy, death-dealing spectres.

Mildred Apsley was placing supper on the table when the clatter of the first pistol shot sent its flat echoes along North Ridge. White-faced, she stood in rigid alarm close to the table. She saw Conant leap out of his chair with a strangely frightening swiftness, grab up his gun-rig from the chair-rail and buckle it about him speedily. That single. echoing shot seemed to spark off a blazing fire in him. With the big Peacemakers belted around his flat-muscled middle, he stood there, his eyes smouldering and his seemingly relaxed body speaking of a dangerous cat-swiftness into which it might leap at any moment.

In spite of her alarm at the sound of the shot from along the ridge, Mead Conant's attitude impressed itself on her:

'*It's the killer in him – his character is written all over him now,*' she heard a small voice inside her say.

Her brother sat frozen in his chair, hands splayed out rigidly on the much-washed tablecloth.

Another pistol shot. And another.

'Come on!' snapped Conant, springing for the door.

'It's along the ridge – Diffin's!' exclaimed Dave Apsley as he came out of his chair and made for the peg on the wall where hung his Smith & Wesson.

Conant tore the door open.

'It's nearer than Diffin's,' he called over his shoulder.

'Must be Quillan's!'

The warm night air swelled into the cabin through the open door. On it rode the crack of a rifle and a spatter of sporadic pistol shots.

'Mildred, take the Winchester an' lock yourself in here,' Dave yelled to his sister. 'If those Flyin' Spur hellions come, keep shootin' until help arrives!'

Mildred nodded and watched her brother race out into the night on the heels of the tall, gun-heavy man who had killer written all over him.

Bill and Seth Diffin heard the first shot as they were loafing in the warm evening, smoking their pipes on the small porch of their homestead.

The brothers turned their faces one to the other, eyes wide, teeth clamped hard on their corn-cob stems. They held the pose for only an instant and the sound of the second pistol crack galvanised them into action.

'It's Quillan's!' grated Seth. 'Them Flyin' Spur slug-throwers are on the loose.'

'Saddle up the cayuses!' snorted his brother, turning quickly towards the door of their dwelling. 'I'll get the guns!'

Within five minutes, Bill and Seth were a-horse and urging their mounts through the dark-wooded slopes of the ridge.

Gerry Hannaway was settled in his rickety rocking-chair perusing a three-week-old copy of the *Tombstone Epitaph* with his glasses balanced on the end of his craggy nose.

The first shot came clattering down the ridge to startle him out of his reading. His wife and daughter gave little squeaks in unison and Tommy, his youngest son, came running in from the yard, the echo of a second shot came in through the door with him.

'*Shootin' along the ridge, Paw!*' yelled the boy urgently.

Hannaway stowed his glasses into a shirt pocket with a philosophic air, folded his paper calmly and stood up, accepting the call to go out and fight as soberly as he accepted the same call at First Bull Run and Chancellorsville when he followed the stars and stripes all those years before.

'Tommy,' he said, 'you an' James take those old rifles of yours, climb up into those two big trees out on the trail an' if anyone lookin' like Flyin' Spur riders come along the trail, fire on 'em. You'll surprise 'em from up there an' they'll have a hard time seein' you, hidden up there. Don't let any of them *hombres* get close to the homestead – it's up to you two to defend your mother an' sister while I'm gone.'

'Where are you goin'?' Hannaway's wife asked.

'Out to fight with my neighbours,' her husband answered levelly, reaching for his Winchester and a box of shells. 'Don't worry none, I'll be back with a whole skin.'

Thoughts whirled through Andy Tyzack's head, mingled with the imaginings of delirium and punctuated with the thunderings of pulsing blood. His body ached dully, his breath soughed heavily and merciless needles of pain stabbed hotly into his chest. He sat the saddle of the toiling pinto with a dogged tenacity, clutching the pommel with both hands and slumping double as if hinged in the middle.

The pinto and the dying man moved slowly up North Ridge, Tyzack striving to utilize his last vestiges of consciousness on guiding the animal to where he knew the Flying Spur gunslingers were lying in wait for Mead Conant.

He had heard shots once but, now, he could hear nothing save the pounding of the blood rushing to his head and the jumbled sounds of delirium.

He hoped that shooting was not the gun-trap, blasting the nester kid who came back as a reputation-pushing gunfighter into the dust.

He sure as blazes had to get up there and make his fight for his kind of folk – nester folk!

Ten

Mead Conant, his bronc pounding along the ridge-top beside that of Dave Apsley, rode in silence with a crimson rage burning high inside him. The gun-fury of Tamblyn's outfit had been unleashed in blazing, barking savagery somewhere along the ridge. The indications were that the shooting came from the Quillan homestead – and he had persuaded the Quillans to stay when they intended running from North Ridge that very day.

If anything had happened to the Quillans, he would never forgive himself.

A gnawing bitterness ate at his innards as he paced his mount along the dark-timbered ridge. There was silence now, an ominous silence following on the clattering heels of the night-echoed shots which spoke of corpses twisted in the dust.

Conant and his companion moved onward in the direction of the Quillan holding, riding swiftly, but with eyes and ears alert in the darkness.

Conant thought of the other nights he had rode a dark trail this day – edged with a tingling apprehen-

97

sion, expecting the white stab of pistol-flame to slash the night and hot drill of a bullet driving into his flesh. There were all too many of those nights in his back-trail. A man got to wonder where it was all to end, even a man with a reputation. In moments of bitter reflection, he saw his ending as being a repetition of the endings of so many of his ilk: a bullet in the back in some dirty, sunbaked cowtown street, a hump of a grave in a boothill cemetery and a crude marker with his name on it and a sardonic epitaph like: 'He was fast, but another was faster!'

It had to be that way, sordid and ignominious – it *just* had to be that way. It was on the cards for all his kind.

The clink of harness gear and the tramp of hooves sounded out of the darkness from where a narrow trail snaked down to the ridge-top trail, splitting the dark stand of liveoaks and aspens.

'Somebody comin'!' whispered Apsley with tense urgency.

They yanked their animals to a halt and sat waiting on the main trail, with hands on the butts of their side-arms.

Two riders came cautiously out of the stand of trees, shadowy, one tall, the other short.

'It's the Diffins!' the nester exclaimed then, in a cautiously raised voice: 'Hey, Bill, Seth! Over here, it's Conant an' Apsley!'

The nester brothers angled their animals out of the narrow trail, moving towards the gunfighter and his companion with hands likewise clutching at their six-gun butts. They eased their mounts through the darkness, leaning inquisitively forward from the saddle with necks craned.

'Yeah, it's you two, all right.' said Bill's voice, satisfied. 'For a minute, we thought you was some of Tamblyn's hellions. What d'you make of it?'

'Hell-raisin' at Quillan's,' Conant said gravely. 'Can't be anyplace else!'

'It's Quillan's, for sure,' rejoined Seth. 'It was too near to be Hannaway's place. It's gone so awful quiet, though – the quiet is worse than the shootin'!'

'Yeah,' grunted the gunfighter. 'Let's vamoose – sittin' our saddle leather an' beatin' our gums ain't goin' to help anyone.'

The four edged their horses along the ridge-trail with a steel-cold apprehension building up in them. The darkness was, as Seth observed, worse than the blazing sounds of gunbattle. The silence and the darkness combined to shroud the high trail with an air of lurking peril. The warm fingers of the night breeze riffled the leaves of the summer-full trees with slight rustlings.

The trail snaked and dipped suddenly into a flat-bottomed gully. High, slab-sided rocks reared on either side with a profusion of tangled trees and shrubbery backing them, growing high to place a dark tracery of leaves against the night sky.

Conant, Apsley and the Diffin brothers came down into the gully, riding with caution.

A stirring in the boles of the trees caused a startled hoot-owl to flutter up against the leaves with hastily beating wings.

The hurried movement of the bird telegraphed a

warning to Mead Conant's brain in a split-second. The owl was not startled by the approach of the four riders, there was something – someone – in the dark cluster of trees whose movement panicked the bird into flight.

Conant hoisted leather, jerking his bronc to a stop.

'Back!' he hissed. 'There's someone in the trees!'

He came out of his saddle with a lightning action, a gun streaking into his right hand as he went. At the very instant his boots slithered, into the dust, a six-gun bellowed out of the dark wall of trees. Conant ducked into a low crouch, marking the position of the flaring muzzle-fire while the slug whined over his hat-crown.

Damn them! he thought. *Only for that owl, they'd have surprised us!*

At his back. Apsley and the Diffin brothers came out of their saddles, clawing at their guns as they moved.

Conant was down in a low gunfighter's crouch on the dark gully floor, both guns in hand and blazing at the position of the hidden gunman as marked by the brief stab of muzzle-flame.

Apsley and the Diffins were casting about in the gloom, seeking cover, when a second gun slammed out of the rocks and trees on the opposite side of the gully and another blazed out from the same direction, blasting its angry bark on the echoes of the first.

Dave Apsley yelled. His yell died in a bubbling gurgle and he pitched face-on into the dust. Conant held his crouch, triggering shots into the dark trees. Muzzle-flames ripped the darkness on both sides of the gully; the whining buzz of flying lead sang through the night and the reeking swirls of cordite smoke choked the gully bottom.

Riderless horses kicked high in panic. Conant pitched himself down behind a small rock, his teeth clenched hard and his Peacemaker Colt hot in his hands.

A sidelong glance showed him that Dave Apsley was sprawled in the dark dust in a crumpled attitude of death. The Diffin brothers were lying on the ground with naked guns smoking in their hands, pressing themselves into the dirt.

'They got Dave, Mead!' came Seth's voice, hoarsed and shocked over the crackle of gunfire that flamed out from the wooded gully sides. 'He's dead!'

Conant hitched himself over on to his back with a quick snake-movement. Leaning his shoulders against the small rock, he began to thumb slugs from his belt-loops into his six-gun chambers.

'Keep down!' he hissed. 'They can't see us too well. I don't know how many are up there in the rocks an' trees. Lie doggo, don't answer their shots from now on and let me make the play.'

The gunhawks in the trees continued slamming shots down into the gully. Seth and Bill Diffin hugged the ground, Conant sprawled behind his rock, making himself as small as possible, holding his guns with tensed trigger fingers.

The cunning with which the guntrap was laid filled him with a numbness he had rarely known before.

We almost rode into it! he told himself. Someone among those blamed Flying Spur gunhands moved too early and set the hoot-owl to flying from the branches.

The warning of the startled bird had been the means of saving the Diffin brothers and he from riding plumb into an ambush. But, they had got Dave Apsley at the outset – cut him down almost before his gun was clear of leather.

That fact gnawed at him with sharp teeth. A throbbing lust for vengeance mounted in him, but he held it down firmly as if keeping the lid on an over-boiling campfire can. He thought of Mildred, who plainly regarded him as a killer and little more. Well, he would kill after this, when the time was ripe, kill to avenge her brother.

The Flying Spur gunhands slashed the night with shots. Dust spouted in dry spurts as slugs ploughed into the dark earth. At the back of the prone, waiting men, their horses clattered away back along the trail, spooked by the blazing gunsong flaming out from the dark stands of rocks and trees.

Still, the three held their silent guns.

'What the hell, Mead?' rasped Bill Diffin, wriggling backwards on his belly. 'Why don't we shoot back? Some of them slugs is comin' mighty close!'

'No!' hissed Conant. 'Hold your fire. Lie quiet, an' make 'em think they plugged us. I want 'em to show themselves.'

The white slashes of muzzle-fire ceased blazing out of the darkness.

Conant lay prone behind the rock, waiting.

The waiting was spiced with a familiar feeling he knew all too well. All emotion, even the nagging yearning to seek vengeance for the killing of Dave

Apsley, drained out of him. There was only waiting, now. An old, tense-edged waiting for the other fellow to show himself.

There was nothing new about the sensation but the location. Conant had known this waiting in many places: in the sun-drenched, hoof-pocked street of a straggling trail-town where he paced the loneliness with hanging hands and a marshal's badge on his coat watched by the populace who peeked around shutters as he went upstreet to meet a gunheavy troublemaker. In the smoke-fogged closeness of a Wyoming saloon, warm after the blizzard outside, into which he walked to face a pair of drunken hellions who stood at the bar with six-guns in their hands. In the wet mud of a horse-corral in a Colorado town where he went to ground, waiting for the young fool who had tried to grab his reputation by throwing a muffed shot at his back in a rainstorm.

Other places than this, many places since he shucked out of Arizona as a fear-numbed nester kid — but the waiting was always the same.

After the last shot echoed away from the sides of the gully, a voice called thinly: 'We got 'em, Luther! Conant an' his *amigos*! I'm goin' down there!'

A voice from the opposite side of the gully answered with the same flat drawl: 'Yeah, but be careful, Brett. Ain't no tellin' if they're lyin' doggo!'

Conant listened to the Texas voices without emotion, his mind going back a matter of three or four months. It was Colorado again where he had stacked his guns against the Bansellings from the Panhandle. He wanted only one, Ace, for the killing of one of his deputies. The Bansellings were clan fighters, however – when you fought one, you fought the whole litter.

In the two minutes of swift-draw-and-blaze, enacted on a sun-pounded flat on the edge of town, he gave Ace Banselling his needings and crippled his brothers. He had been a fool. The surviving Texas clansmen would stick together and make the seeking of vengeance the prime motive of living their lives, he should have known that.

So, the Bansellings were here.

And he was waiting.

He lay in the dust, thumbing back the hammers of his guns.

With a detached portion of his mind, he reflected that there were more than the two brothers up there on either side of the gully; they had a bunch of Flying Spur gunnies with them and the game would have to be played cautiously. He must play it alone, too, utilising the skill and knowledge garnered in the many tight spots he had known as his trigger-reputation stacked higher.

Figures came down out of the trees and off the rocks, distant, shadowed and half-emerged with the darkness of the night. A harsh voice was raised gleefully: 'Hey – we sure enough fixed 'em, there ain't no sign of 'em!'

The Texas drawl of a Banselling answered: 'Yeah!'

The group of men were coming cautiously along the darkened gully towards where Conant and the two nesters sprawled silent in the dust, the slow ring of their spurs accompanying their careful onward march.

'Hold it!' whispered Conant to his companions. 'I'll make the play!'

The Flying Spur men drew nearer, six of them, two of them, even at this distance and in the darkness, recognisable as the lank, loose-boned Banselling brothers, walking onward, each carrying two drawn guns.

Then, Seth and Bill Diffin saw Conant move into swift action.

He came up from the ground like an uncoiling spring in the very faces of the oncoming Flying Spur men.

The Peacemaker Colts in his hands blazed white flame as Conant, in a gunfighter's crouch, went into a swiftly whirling Dervish dance. The gully resounded with the clattering slam of the barking guns. In the reeking swirls of thickening smoke the dim figures of men crumpled to the ground.

Sprawling in the dust, the Diffin brothers watched the big gunfighter cut down the hostile Flying Spur wranglers, moving in his swift dance, making every shot tell.

Voices yelled in panic, over the bellowing Colts. Through the veils of drifting gunsmoke, the obscure figures of running men were visible, hastening away from the one-man onslaught. The crumpled forms of dead Flying Spur trigger-slicks lay on the dark earth. One of the Bansellings, gunless, was moving aimlessly around the gully floor on his hands and knees, clutching his middle, struggling against gusty sighs to call in a choking voice after the remainder of the would-be bushwhackers running away along the gully at his back: '*Brett – he plugged me – don't leave me – damn you, Brett—!*'

Conant stood spraddle-legged, a big and misty figure with whirls of gunsmoke wreathing around him. He watched Luther Banselling, cursing, gurgling, slowly folding down to join the remainder of the dead men on the ground. There was only the pulsing desire for vengeance in him now, a throbbing lust to square with Tamblyn's outfit for the killing of Apsley and for whatever had happened at the Quillan homestead where there had been shooting and now was silence.

Luther Banselling flopped to the earth with the beginnings of a death rattle gagging his throat. The brothers Diffin came upright and stood at his back.

'Doggone,' breathed Bill in wonderment. 'Now I know how you got that big reputation – you were faster'n a sidewinder!'

'You two boys run back a ways an' catch our cayuses,' Conant said flatly. 'I'm goin' up the gully to chase those galoots that ran. There's one of 'em I want specially.'

Seth and Bill went back along the gully in search of the spooked horses, Conant moved forward cautiously then halted to stare along the night-shrouded stretch of the gully while he pushed slugs into the empty chambers of his six-guns, working by touch. There was an ominous stillness and tranquillity along there where Brett Banselling and the other fleeing gunmen had vanished into the darkness.

The gunfighter began to progress cautiously along the dark sweep of the gully. He could not see far ahead and did not know whether or not other gunhands lurked along the rockstrewn and tree-grown sides. He had moved forward for a matter of fifty yards when there was a sudden scuffling movement ahead in the darkness.

He saw two figures come leaping out of the gloom as if the gully sides had given birth to them. He was aware of the six-guns in their hands and his own weapons came up with the spontaneity of reflex-action, triggering out blades of muzzle-flame to slash the night.

One of the dark figures went falling stiffly backwards, his hat jerking from his head as he went down. The second fired his gun the very instant he went into a tangle-footed forward tumble, the slug whanged past Conant's head, ploughing a stinging furrow in his cheek. The gunfighter sprang sidewise, his feet encountered loose shale and he slithered off to one side, falling heavily, unable to prevent himself from doing so. He gave a hoarse, involuntary squawk as the wound inflicted in his arm by Arch Tamblyn's men on Moroni Creek jarred with sickening pain against a rock. A needle of agony stabbed the whole length of his arm and a Peacemaker went spinning from his numbed fingers.

He closed his eyes against the white blur of pain, lay gasping with his mouth wide open in an agonized twist.

There came a low and sinister laugh.

Mead Conant opened his eyes. Through a blur of salty tears, he saw the big figure of Brett Banselling looming large out of the gloom, astonishingly near and with naked guns outlined in his hands.

The Texas gunman was laughing malevolently and with evil relish.

He was going to take his time about it.

Eleven

Mead Conant squirmed in the dust, gritting his teeth against the jarring sear of the pain in his arm and trying to raise his remaining gun before the lank Texan fired. For the first time in his gunfighting career, he found himself curiously slow; strength seemed to be ebbing from him and the conception of that boot-hill grave with the sardonic epitaph impressed itself distinctly upon his consciousness.

Things happened speedily, but with the appearance of slowness. Even as he brought up the gun with a strangely leaden arm, he saw the remaining brother of the Banselling clan level his twin Colts. Another laugh grated from the shadowy form of the Texan.

An indistinct black blob moved in the gloom at Brett Banselling's back; the clink of a hoof sounded on hard rock, followed by the blast of a gun and the brief snarl of a bullet.

Brett Banselling scooted forward on his toes in a wooden pose. One of the fingers that had been in the act of tightening on a trigger to slam a slug into the sprawling form of Conant loosed an ineffective shot into the dust. Then, the Texas gunman toppled as stiff as a felled tree and smote the earth face-on with a meaty thud.

Conant shook his head like a man coming suddenly out of a dream. The flat drifts of gunsmoke stung his eyes, but he perceived an indistinct form beyond the hazy curtain – the form of a man, slumped along a pinto's back, clutching a smoking six-gun. Conant hauled himself out of the dust and stumbled through the pall of swirling smoke. His jarred arm ached with a nagging persistence and the bullet-furrow in his cheek throbbed with stinging pain.

From the saddle of the pinto pony which had appeared so suddenly at Banselling's back, Andy Tyzack regarded the gunfighter with dim eyes.

'Glad I was able to help you, Conant,' he said in a gasping voice. 'I tried to get up – here to warn you about the Flyin' Spur – an' the Quillans; but them blasted Texas gunnies shot me down an' left me for dead on the trail.' The sheriff of Huajillo County spoke with a failing voice, punctuated by spells of painful wheezing.

'The Quillans!' exclaimed Conant. 'What about the Quillans?'

'Tamblyn loosed his hellions on the Quillan homestead – so you would ride out to help the Quillans – plumb into this gully where the – Banselling brothers an' some others were waitin' to, gun you. I figured it was time I quit bein' a drunken hound-dog, jumpin' to Tamblyn's say-so, so I lit out. Figured it was time I did – somethin' for my own kind of folk – nester folk!'

'You did somethin', all right, Andy,' praised Conant.

'You couldn't have showed up when you were more needed. Banselling was fixin' to kill me an' he had me at a disadvantage.'

'Ain't much further use, I guess,' breathed the wounded man with difficulty. 'I'm goin' fast – watch out for the rest of them Flyin' Spur hellions – the whole bunch is somewhere along the ridge—' Tyzack's faint voice died in a choking cough and his crouched body became limp over the saddle-horn. His last breath whistled out of him gustily.

Bill and Seth Diffin came out of the gloom, round-eyed and leading the three horses.

'What in hell happened?' demanded Seth.

'Andy Tyzack here showed up an' plugged Brett Banselling right when he was commencing to ventilate me,' Conant informed him. 'He was half dead because the Bansellings met him on the trail an' cut him down. He was tryin' to get up here to give us a warnin' about the Flyin' Spur raid. Andy was all right – he was a nester!'

Bill Diffin breathed a low oath. 'The number of times I cursed him for bein' a no-good barfly an' a Flyin' Spur bootlicker,' he commented.

Conant paced the dark ground to reclaim his lost gun and found it close to the stiffening form of Brett Banselling.

'There's no time to bury Apsley or Tyzack,' he said gravely. 'Lay Tyzack in the brush an' turn his pony loose. He tried to tell me about a raid on the Quillan place an' said the whole Flyin' Spur crew was on the rampage along the ridge.'

After the frenzied shooting, a deep and eerie silence

had settled on North Ridge, fraught with edgy apprehension.

'Quillan's place was attacked as a means of gettin' us to ride into a gun-trap here. Those Bansellings wanted me because I shot their brother in Colorado,' Mead Conant stated. 'The trail between here and the Quillan holdin' is probably thick with Tamblyn's rannies. Can we get there any other way?'

'We can move through the trees along the west side of this gully and come out close to Quillan's place,' Bill answered. 'It'll be rough goin' with the horses.'

'We'll lead 'em,' Conant said. 'C'mon.'

The trio led the horses up the now silent, tree studded sweep of the gully side. The going was, as Bill had warned, rough. The animals slithered on the shaly and rock-strewn slopes, but the men steadied them.

Even as they entered the trees, they heard the drumming of many hooves sounding, along the dark gully from the west. Conant and his companions pulled the horses to a halt and stood in the gloom-shrouded trees.

The hoof-thumps grew louder and the fickle moon slithered from behind a scurrying cloud-bank to silver a jostling bunch of big-hatted riders entering the gully. Above the tramp of the hurrying horses, they heard the raspy voice of Arch Tamblyn yelling with a triumphant note:

'The shooting's over – they must have ventilated Conant for sure!'

'It sounded like some battle,' observed a wrangler from the midst of the mounted bunch.

'He probably had some of them snivellin' nesters

with him,' rejoined the gravelly voice of Tamblyn. 'If them Bansellings an' the rest of the boys wiped out the whole stinkin' bunch at one throw, then it's *muy bueno* an' North Ridge is sure enough cow-country!' The observation gave way to a yell, Tamblyn calling on the Bansellings and the rest of the bushwhackers as he yanked his horse to a halt: 'Hey, you Texas *hombres* an' the rest of you! Where in blazes are you?'

Conant, Bill and Seth held a silent pose in the darkness of the clustered trees. They heard boots crunch on the shaly ground down in the gully and a voice, high with unbelief, called: 'Hey, Arch, Brett Banselling is here – dead. An' there's a couple of others here an' Andy Tyzack!'

Arch Tamblyn's drawled curses came thick and loud from the gully bottom.

'Them blamed, dirt-rakin' nesters! They finished off our bunch!'

A rumble of incredulous profanity reached the ears of the men in the trees. Then, Tamblyn bellowed: 'Conant an' the rest of that flea-bitten crowd must be somewhere close! Spread out an' find 'em; after we get through with 'em, we'll raze every nester roost on the ridge – Apsley's, the Diffins' an that Yank's on the far edge of the ridge!'

The mounted Flying Spur men began to jostle into action as the moon floated behind a cloud.

'What now?' asked Seth Diffin. 'They're spreadin' all along the ridge!'

'We'll have to dig ourselves down some place an' make a stand against 'em – the whole bunch of us, concentrated in one spot. Gerry Hannaway's is the best place, it's the last homestead they'll reach. Let's find out what happened at Quillan's, then move on to Hannaway's.' At the back of his mind, a disturbing thought was intensifying to disturb Conant. Trouble-hungry Flying Spur hellions were moving along the ridge in all directions – and Mildred Apsley was completely alone in the last homestead at the further-most eastern end. She was isolated and the gun-heavy Tamblyn riders were spreading between them.

Silently, they moved through the trees to eventually break their cover, bringing their led horses slithering down a loose-surfaced rise and finding the neat Quillan homestead standing a matter of yards to their fore.

The screech of a frightened child shrilled from the lamplit homestead. Conant and the Diffin brothers moved cautiously around the side of the small build-ing into the once neat yard and stopped in their tracks as the sight illumined by the yellow lamplight bloom-ing from the open door met their eyes.

The pathetic form of Becky Quillan was stretched dead in the yellow dirt, holding a Winchester in a stiff and slender hand. Carl was curled up in a grotesque position by the buggy which he had loaded that very day in readiness to move off the ridge.

The Diffins whispered jagged oaths. Conant stood regarding the bodies of the homesteader couple, a cold numbness mounting in him. He was to blame for this as much as those Flying Spur trigger-slicks. A bitter, taunting voice whispered inside his skull:

'You talked them into staying today! They might have been clear away by this time, but for you! And

you're the slick-talking gun-toter who promised them no harm would come to them!'

A movement from the open door of the homestead caused the jibing voice to cease as Conant whirled around, a hand clawing for a gun.

He saw a tall figure, backed by the lemon lamplight, appear in the doorway. A Winchester barrel glittered with a yellow sheen and a flat, northerner's voice said: *'You murderin' hogs!'*

Bill Diffin's voice yipped: 'Gerry! Hold it – it's us!'

Conant lowered the Peacemaker that was already clear of leather and levelled. The spraddle-legged figure in the doorway moved forward, reflected lamplight deepening the furrows of Gerry Hannaway's Lincolnesque face.

'Doggone,' husked Hannaway. 'I thought you were some of the Flyin' Spur butchers coming back!'

He lowered the repeater and joined the trio.

'I came out as soon as I heard shots. When I got here, the Tamblyn crew was just pullin' out. I saw it wasn't any use tryin' to make a fight against 'em, so I hid in the trees 'til they went. When I found Carl an' Becky dead, I went in to quieten the kids. Three kids in there, Conant, an' their maw an' paw dead in the dirt. I never knowed anythin' like this – not even in the war!'

'We'll even up with 'em,' promised Conant without emotion. 'Is everythin' safe at your place?'

'Yeah, as far as I know. I planted my two boys up in a couple of big trees overlookin' the trail. They can surprise anyone who rides that way plumb easy. I heard no shots from that direction, but there was all hell soundin' from along the ridge a few minutes back. I figured they'd swooped on the Diffins' place.'

'That was us,' Conant told him. 'They tried to pull a dry-gulch play, but it blew up in their faces – Apsley was killed, though.'

'Hell,' snorted Hannaway.

The mention of Dave Apsley brought Conant's thoughts to his sister.

'Listen, Gerry, we've got to make a stand somewhere, the whole bunch of us, an' your place seems to be the only place right now. You an' Bell an' Seth get along there *pronto* an' hole up – take the Quillan youngsters with you for your wife an' daughters to care for.'

'Where are you goin'?' queried Seth.

'Back along the ridge to get Mildred Apsley; she's alone in the homestead an' the Flyin' Spur gunnies are movin' that way!'

He hooked a boot into the stirrup of his bronc and said, as he forked his long legs over the saddle: 'I'll join you later.'

In his brain, the sardonic voice added: *If I'm lucky!*

Twelve

Dawn came red and raw over the summer-thick leaves of the wooded ridge.

Conant, riding eastward off the main ridge-trail, paced his bronc steadily through the trees and became aware of a flickering redness that was not the hue of the dawn filtering through the cluttered boles. As he moved a hundred yards onward, the acrid and hot reek of burning wood drifted to him. The whoop of devilishly gleeful voices came to his ears.

'They're busy burnin' the Diffins' homestead,' he grunted, slapping his knees into the ribs of the bronc, urging it to a quicker progress through the thickly clustered trees.

He recalled Arch Tamblyn's voice yelling his intention to raze all the homesteads on North Ridge. As if prompted by Conant's thought, the rancher's voice sounded through the red-flushed trees: 'That's a tolerable blaze, now for Apsley's place!'

Conant set his teeth grimly. The Flying Spur marauders would take the ridge-trail; he would have to keep angling eastward through the trees and just keep on hoping he would reach the homestead and Mildred ahead of them. He kept pacing the horse at the fastest speed he could urge out of it on a journey so impeded by trees, putting the filtering blaze of the Diffin holding behind him while dawn widened in the vast sky. He heard a distant thump of hooves and clink of harness-gear and a whoop of savage glee, denoting that the Flying Spur hellions were saddled up and moving towards the Apsley holding – and Mildred.

Conant, a bleak-eyed apparition in the swelling light of dawn, heeled sharp spur-rowells into his bronc's hide. The searing bullet-furrow in his cheek throbbed hotly and the jarred wound in his arm ached dully.

He moved the horse through the wooded slopes like a madman; low sprouting twigs whipped across his face, stinging briefly as he threaded the stands of trees.

He reached the ridge-trail ahead of the Flying Spur riders now converging on the Apsley homestead and at a point only a matter of yards from the Apsley holding. Putting the bronc into a snorting run, he went into the yard of the homestead in a whirl of dust, hoping that Mildred, would not take him for a Tamblyn rider and pump a Winchester slug into him.

No snarling slug came his way as he reined the bronc to a slithering halt abreast of the window. He saw Mildred's drawn features appear behind the small panes of the aperture, her mouth dropping open in sudden shock. He reflected in a detached manner that he would present no pleasing spectacle to appear suddenly at a window, with his bullet-ridged cheek from which drying blood streaked clear down his face and neck.

He cupped his hands to the window.

'It's me, Mildred,' he called. 'Come outside – quick! Don't waste any time, Tamblyn's bunch are on their way here!'

Mildred moved away from the window. The metallic slither of a drawn bolt sounded from the door and it swung open. She came out, carrying the Winchester.

'What's the matter?' she demanded. She was pale, but obviously fighting to hold back her panic. 'I've heard shooting all along the ridge—'

'No time for talk,' cut in Conant curtly. 'They burned the Diffin place an' they're on their way here. Jump up behind me!'

The girl obeyed, clutching the repeater and hoisting herself to the rear of the gunfighter's saddle, the skirts of her simple homesteader dress swirling.

Conant wheeled the horse about, making for the way he came.

Mildred said: 'Where's Dave?'

Conant felt a drag at his heart and ignored the question.

'We're makin' for Hannaway's place,' he told her over the thump of the dust-raising hooves of the bronc. 'The homesteaders are holin' up there to make a fight of it. It's the last place Tamblyn an' his crew will reach. We'll have to go by way of the trees. It's a long detour, but the only way.'

They rounded a sweep in the ridge-trail and Conant urged the bronc up the slope giving on to the wooded top of the ridge. Even as they went up, Mildred cast a glance over her shoulder and saw a wide banner of dust spiralling and growing larger in the broadening light of the new day.

The drumming tattoo of hooves sounded low, then grew louder rapidly.

The double-burdened bronc toiled into the trees. Conant paused, once in the thick of the boles, to allow the animal to catch its wind. He looked back with the girl. Because of the sweeping turn of the ridge-trail, the homestead was hidden from this point, but the yells of the Flying Spur men could be heard plainly. Harsh laughter cackled up to them and someone loosed a playful shot. A sinister glee was running high in Tamblyn's gun-hung wranglers now.

Conant yipped up the bronc, heading its nose into the midst of the wooded ridge-crest.

After little more than half-an-hour of steady riding during which they circled the smoking remains of the Diffin homestead, they dismounted to give the horse a blow. Mildred leaned against the bole of a live-oak. her eyes fixed on a thick ribbon of smoke hazing above the trees from the eastern end of the ridge, smoke which did not come from the Diffin holding.

Conant followed her gaze and he watched the swell of smoke in silence, thinking of the place Dave Apsley had toiled so hard to build going up in smoke at the hands of Tamblyn's hellions. He remembered that night, twelve years before, when his father's homestead went the same way.

You sure could not teach old dogs like Tamblyn new tricks: they went on performing the old ones every time.

As if she read his thoughts touching on her brother, the girl said: 'You wouldn't answer me when I asked about Dave. He's dead, isn't he?' Her voice was level, without hint of tears.

Conant faced her. There was no point in concealing the truth any longer.

'Yeah, he's dead,' he replied softly, 'an' Becky an' Carl Quillan an' old Andy Tyzack, who turned up trumps at the finish.'

He saw Mildred's strained face, circled with its halo of spun-gold hair, harden slightly. He felt strangely disturbed at that. He did not want her personality to be hurt, or her appearance marked by what was happening here – but he knew it was inevitable, just as his own personality had been hardened by what happened on Moroni Creek.

Still, there was no sign of tears from the nester girl. She simply repeated the names incredulously: '*Becky and Carl, as well, and that poor old sheriff!*' Then, in a steady voice. she added: 'Now I know what turned you into a gunfighter. Feeling as I do now, I could become one myself!'

It was strange, this change in her, when weighed against the sight of the tearful girl who, so very recently, derided him as a wanton killer after hearing of his brash visit to the Flying Spur. Strange and a little frightening.

He knew what she meant by saying she could become a gunfighter herself. His life had been moulded and cast in the turmoil loosed on the Moroni Creek homestead by Tamblyn twelve years ago. He never shot down a lawbreaker without the thought that he was shooting down a Tamblyn man running through his mind. Every hellion who ever shucked a six-gun from leather was, in Conant's mind, associated with those who rode on the Conant homestead. Every slug he ever slammed into a saddle-bandit was a slug for his father, Clay and Lloyd.

'Let's travel,' he urged, breaking his own reverie. 'We have a tolerable distance to go an' this ridge is no place to linger.'

They climbed on to the bronc again and went cautiously along the timbered ridge-top, riding in silence with the gunfighter urging all possible speed out of the steed. Behind them, echoing thinly now, they still heard the whoops and raucous yells of Tamblyn's riders. The snorting bronc crested the highest point of the timberline and Conant turned it westward in a loop which would bring them to the Hannaway place.

After coming down the far side of the crest to a narrow trail which snaked in the direction of Hannaway's homestead, they met trouble.

No sooner had Conant turned the double-burdened animal on to the trail than a whoop, raised against a concentrated throb of pounding hooves, sounded behind them. A hasty glance showed Conant that a small knot of riders were drumming around a twist in the trail, plumes of dust clouding behind them, sparkled by the brilliance of the blazing morning sunshine. One of the riders gave a loud cry and the speed of the oncoming mounts increased.

Conant cursed behind clenched teeth and kicked his spurs into the flanks of the overloaded bronc in a

desperate effort to urge more speed out of the snorting, toiling animal.

Those Flying Spur rannihans must have split into
two bunches and this detachment was headed for
Hannaway's homestead by way of this back trail.
Normally, he could swivel around in the saddle as he
rode and throw bullets at them but, as it was, with the
girl clinging to his back, he was helpless. The Tamblyn
riders knew it, too, and were increasing their speed.

A snarling shot whanged out of the bunch of hotly
pursuing riders and streaked past the heads of the
man and girl.

Conant was about to grab for a six-gun and make
an effort to shoot back as best he could with the hand-
icap of the girl clinging to his back when the deafening blast of a carbine sounded inches away from his
ear. He turned his head and saw that Mildred was
clinging to the pony with her knees alone, was twisted
about and held the Winchester to her shoulder with a
grey ribbon of smoke dribbling from its mouth into the
wind. A pursuing Flying Spur gunhand was clutching
his middle and bawling a stream of profanity. Conant
heard the sharp click of another round being pumped
into the Winchester and Mildred said calmly: 'Keep
going. I'll keep shooting.'

The gunfighter spur-raked the bronc mercilessly. If
anyone ever told him, he reflected, that he would ride
double with a girl while she pegged shots at pursuing
gunslingers he would have laughed in their faces.
Still, here he was in that situation – and it was one
lone Winchester against a pack of trigger-slick guns,
for it was impossible for him to find a clear aim owing

to the presence of the girl. They could not survive against those kind of odds, any more than this winded, double-loaded bronc could outrun the pursuing horses – they just could not.

The Flying Spur bunch loosed a hail of shots just as Conant and the homesteader girl rode the bronc down a declivity and around a shoulder of high, cactus studded rock and sand. The angry leaden hornets zipped past them, peppering the air at a spot where their heads had been just before the bronc rounded the turn.

'They didn't touch us!' exclaimed Mildred in astonishment. She brought the Winchester up again as Conant bloodied his spur rowels, making along the stretch of trail alongside which the house, barn and pole-fenced hog-pen of Gerry Hannaway's homestead stood.

Mildred fired again as the first rider of the pursuing knot rounded the shoulder and came into full view. By accident rather than design, she took his horse in its head and the animal sprawled to the dusty trail, its legs splaying four directions at once. The rider went whirling from his saddle. The fallen horse and rider caused a chaotic pile-up of the madly riding bunch.

Conant reached the yard of the Hannaway holding feeling he bore a charmed life – maybe his passenger brought him luck, he mused. He yanked rein on the weary bronc in a flurry of flying dust, vaguely aware of faces contemplating their arrival from the window of the Hannaway home and that the pile-up uptrail was sorting itself out and the Tamblyn riders were coming down on the homestead like bats out of hell.

He came out of the saddle as if it had suddenly become red-hot and hauled Mildred Apsley from the bronc's back none too gently. He shoved the Winchester wielding girl in the direction of the house.

'Get in there,' he ordered. 'It's my turn to shoot!'

Mildred hastened for the door which someone was already opening and Mead Conant turned to face the approaching Flying Spur wranglers. Those watching from the cabin did not perceive his hands move for his holsters – they were simply full of Peacemaker Colt all of a sudden, as if by some magical act.

Seth and Bill Diffin once more witnessed his peculiar gunfighter's dance as he went into action out there in the homestead yard. He began triggering shots with both guns, making each tell by dropping one of the oncoming marauders from his saddle. Such was the swiftness of his nimble-footed dance that no two shots were fired from the same spot.

Leaving half a dozen crumpled forms in their wake, the riders hauled their mounts around and headed back the way they came.

Conant stood in a gunfighter's crouch in the yard, watching their dwindling backs through a kicked-up haze of dust.

He was under no false impressions. They would be back – the whole hell-begotten crew of them!

Thirteen

Conant took the weary bronc into Hannaway's barn, hitching it to a rail and hastening towards the homestead. Someone opened the door of the cabin and he entered to join Hannaway, his family, the Diffin brothers and Mildred. The wife and daughter of Hannaway were soothing the Quillan children and the lean Northerner slapped the gunfighter heartily on the back as he entered.

'Nice shootin', Mead,' he declared lustily. 'I never see a feller go into action the way you did – you set them Tamblyn hellions to high-tailin' like a mountain lion chousin' a hound-dog!'

'Better dig yourselves in for a siege,' Conant answered flatly. 'They'll be back, the whole bunch of 'em, an' they'll take some fightin'.'

Seth Diffin pushed hot coffee into the gunfighter's hand and Conant drank it gratefully, realising for the first time how long he had been without food and drink. As he drank, he gazed from the small window of the homestead, noting the two high pines, rearing summer-profuse greenery against the blue sky, one on either side of the trail outside.

'Those the trees where you planted your boys, Gerry?' he asked.

'Yeah, there's good cover in the top of 'em an' you can look right down on the trail,' Hannaway replied.

Conant rubbed his blue-bristled chin thoughtfully.

'You can dominate the whole trail by puttin' a couple of men with Winchesters up there in the pines,' he mused aloud, 'unless the Flyin' Spur riders come on the homestead from some other direction.'

'They can't,' Hannaway told him, 'that's the only way they can approach this holdin' – along that trail an' between those two trees.'

'Then we can hold 'em off. I think we can stop 'em from burnin' yore homestead, at least, Gerry. You a good hand with a Winchester?'

'Tolerable,' the homesteader answered. 'Come out with me an' we'll get ourselves up there in the pines. The rest of you, Seth, Bill, an' you Hannaway boys, stand close to this window an' keep yore guns trained on the trail, right between those two trees. If this works out, the chances are we'll finish off the Tamblyn crew before they get around to butcherin' us.'

Mildred Apsley, gripping her own Winchester, moved to the single window in company with the nesters.

'You better stay back there with the rest of the women,' Conant told her.

The nester girl shook her head.

'Not me, I turned gunfighter, too – remember?'

Conant quirked a hard grin of admiration at her spirit as he left the homestead with Gerry Hannaway.

'If we get them gunnies halted between the two

trees, they'll be plumb in yore range,' he called back to the defenders of the little house. 'Let 'em have it before they start shootin' on you!'

There was a distinct eeriness in the sun-charged air as Conant and Hannaway moved across the dusty homestead yard towards the twin pines.

'What do you aim to do?' queried the homesteader.

'If we get ourselves concealed up there in the tree-tops, we can hold Tamblyn's bunch off with ease, keepin' 'em back from the house. Any one of 'em who gets past our barrage will be in full view of the window an' one of those in the house can pick him off.'

'Seems like it might work, too,' grunted the lean and gaunt nester, turning his head to appraise the distance between the trees flanking the trail and the window of the house.

He saw the face of Mildred Apsley gazing out of the window and the sun, shining on to the small pane, glinted on the Winchester in her hand.

'That Apsley girl,' Hannaway grunted. 'I never figured she'd take up a gun that way.'

'Nor did I,' Mead Conant answered. 'The other day she called me a man-killer – figured I had no right to gun down trigger-slicks. Now that her own brother's been killed by the Tamblyn bunch, she's changed her opinion an' got herself some of the gunfighter spirit.'

'Good for her,' commented Hannaway.

'I'm not so sure it is,' the other replied gravely. 'I know what the gunfighter spirit is – I've been fightin' to get free of it since I was a kid. It twists you, Gerry – even if you trip yore triggers on the side of the law. Sometimes you get to thinkin' yore bigger than the law just because you can unleather yore iron faster than some others. I don't like to see a woman go that way!'

Hannaway gave a grunt.

They were at the trees. They clicked the safety catches of their repeaters, shoved them into their waistbelts and began to climb the pines. Soon, they were high in the thickly bunched needles of greenery. Each squatted on a thick limb where he was hidden from the trail below, but could look down upon it through apertures in the foliage.

'As soon as they show themselves on the trail, get your rifle ready an' pick 'em off if they don't halt when I yell to 'em,' Conant directed, calling to Hannaway, in his tree on the opposite margin of the trail.

They waited a tension-edged twenty minutes, crouching in the thick, sweet-smelling branches of the high trees. Then, the distant drumming of many hooves sounded, its thumping slowly growing into a loud tattoo.

'Here they come the whole blasted bunch of 'em by the sound of 'em!' Conant called. 'Don't rush it, Gerry, let 'em get right close.'

Around the rock and sand shoulder hunching into the bend of the trail ahead, came a dust-stirring clutter of wide-hatted horsemen. There was no mistaking the paunchy figure riding to the fore. The whole of the Flying Spur's force of slug-throwers were bearing down on the Hannaway holding, with the man who paid them bullet-money in the lead.

Squatting in his tree, Gerry Hannaway heard the sharp rasp of a Winchester breech-pump snap across from the pine in which the gunfighter straddled.

'Hold it now, Gerry,' came the slow and calculating voice of Conant.

Through a space in the clustered pine-needles. Conant levelled his repeater, covering a spot on the trail some twenty yards from the pines, full in the path of the oncoming raiders. He waited until the Flying Spur wranglers thundered nearer, then triggered a snapping shot down to the trail, causing a spurt of dry dust to fountain up in the path of Arch Tamblyn's mount as the slug spanged into the trail.

Cursing, the rancher reared back his horse into a slithering halt, the riders at his back following suit.

'Where the blue blazes did that come from?' bellowed the spiky-moustached Flying Spur owner.

'Up here!' shouted Conant. 'We got Winchesters levelled on you, Tamblyn! Better haul yore cayuses around an' get the hell off this ridge!'

The old Texan gave a grating and mirthless laugh, then spat out a filthy oath.

'You're talkin' plumb foolish, Conant,' he roared. 'This is the last homestead on the ridge an' we aim to shoot it up! An' we'll trigger you out of that tree like a jay-bird, too!'

'Try it,' invited Conant.

Tamblyn flourished the Colt he gripped in his hand in a wave of encouragement to his men.

'Come on boys!' he yipped. 'Let's smoke out these lousy nesters!'

The Flying Spur riders spurred up their horses to move forward between the twin pines guarding the trail.

Conant and Hannaway fired at once, dropping two from their saddles, but the bunch of raiders came onward. They came between the two trees, full into the aim of the watching nesters at the small window of the homestead. At once, a fusillade of shots crackled out and two more Flying Spur riders dropped to the trail.

Tamblyn and his followers yanked their horses around in slithering turns, thoroughly panicked. They hustled back through the sentinel pines, firing wild shots over their shoulders as they went. Tamblyn howled a raucous order for them to turn and try another attack. They did so, throwing some wild shots up at the pair concealed in the pines as they returned down the trail.

Conant dropped one rider with a shot while Gerry Hannaway sent a horse sprawling wide-legged into the dust, its rider being flung into a heap beside the trail.

Between the pines went the raiders, once more to be greeted with a blazing hail of lead from the defenders of the homestead. Tamblyn's hat was snatched from his head and another rider and horse went crumpling to the ground.

They retreated again in a jostling, pounding disorder of whinneying animals and cursing men. Two more shots from Conant and Hannaway sped them on their way back along the trail.

Fifty yards from the trees, they settled themselves into some form of order, pulling their horses around to face the object of their attack once more. One dark-faced rider was clutching a wounded hand, he shouted:

'It's no use, Arch, they got us to right!'

'No they ain't,' rasped the grating tones of Tamblyn. 'It's them buzzards in the pines! They're puttin' the halter on us afore we get close to the nester roost — gun 'em out an' the rest'll be easy!'

'Can't see 'em,' another voice said. 'They're up in the branches an' the sun's right back of the trees — it nearly blinds you to look up there!'

'The hell with that!' bellowed Tamblyn. 'Give 'em hot slugs!'

He touched spurs to his mount, urging the animal forward and, flourishing his six-gun, came upon the twin pines once more, with his riders at his back.

Up in the branches, Conant and Hannaway fired, loaded and fired again. More Flying Spur raiders dropped from their saddles. Their wildly directed shots slashed through the pine-needles without harming the two riflemen and another withering burst of Winchester fire from the defenders of the homestead caused them to turn tail once more, leaving a further three of their number sprawled on the trail.

The now diminished group of riders halted once more, out of Winchester range of the men concealed in the high pines. Arch Tamblyn's voice was raised in lurid oaths.

'By grab, you flea-bitten dirt-rakers, I'll run you off this ridge yet!' he railed, shaking his fist in the general direction of the Hannaway homestead. A group of riders pulled away from the main bunch, following the lead of tho dark-faced man with the injured hand.

'Where the blue blazes are you goin'?' roared Tamblyn, turning to face them.

'Twenty-seven miles away from here,' retorted the dark-faced one. 'We know when we're bottled up, Tamblyn, an' yore gun-wages aren't high enough to push us into that gun-trap again!'

Arch Tamblyn almost leaped out of his El Paso saddle. That quirk of cold fear he first knew when Conant rode into the Flying Spur's yard with the remains of Spade Lacy over his bronc's back needled at his innards once more. They were running out on him. It was the same play Kersands, Millick, Heldkopf and Wilkes had made — yellow, the whole damned bunch of them!

'You lily-livered Gentle Annies!' thundered the owner of the Flying Spur. 'You let a bunch of dirt grub-bin', corn-plantin' nesters bulldog you. I thought you were gunslingin' cowmen!'

'So we are, but we let a bunch of dirt-grubbin', corn-plantin' nesters bulldog us this easy when they do it so well. Take a look at how many of yore men are dead in the dust, Tamblyn,' snorted he of the dark features. 'Yore gun-money ain't worth it — nobody's gun-money is worth it!'

Loudly, Arch Tamblyn took a verbal trek over the badlands of profanity.

Two or three of the riders who were ranged around him sidled their horses across the trail to join the knot surrounding the dark-featured one. One of them said:

'Rose is right, Arch, Yore fight's over. It's that Conant who's fazed the whole thing. The play he made against that Banselling pair an' the other galoots back there in the gully, the way he met us in that home-stead yard yonder after we chased him an' the girl, an' the way he's rigged this trick here prove you can't buck against an *hombre* like him. He's plumb hell on wheels an' you can fight him on yore lonesome if you've a mind – we're hightailin'!'

Tamblyn, with the cold qualm of fear building inside him, suddenly became more aware than ever that he was becoming an old man. He sat his saddle in silence for a moment with a small group of faithful riders cluttered about him. Then he rounded on those who had ranged themselves on the side of the dark-faced one.

'You're a lousy crowd of yeller-bellied saddle-tramps!' he howled. 'You can take yoreselves off to blazes! I can run off these sodbusters an' Conant on my solo lonesome, if I have to! I got another ace up my sleeve that ain't been played yet!'

The dark-featured rider kicked spurs to the flanks of his horse and turned the animal's nose to face the eastern snaking trail. He pivoted his body in his saddle with a creak of leather and hooted a jeering laugh at the Texan.

'Let's hope it's a better ace than Ace Banselling's brothers from the Panhandle, Tamblyn – it'll need to be to lick that Conant *hombre*!' A rattle of laughter was raised by the rest of the deserting men as they turned their animals to follow that of the dark faced one, now headed on the out-trail.

'*Adios*, Tamblyn,' called one. 'We figger we'd sooner stick to wranglin' cows, peaceable-like, 'stead of throwin' our gunhands into yore fight!'

Conant and Hannaway watched from the trees as the dark faced man and his riders moved off along the ridge, leaving Tamblyn with no more than half a dozen riders mounted around him.

The rancher and his remaining men watched the dark faced rider and his adherents take their horses along the trail at a brisk canter and disappear around the hunching shoulder of sand and rock around which the trail curved.

As the drifting banner of their dust settled to the ground, Tamblyn yanked his horse around to face the homestead and the trees which sheltered Conant and Hannaway. He sat his saddle, well out of Winchester range, his horse kicking up small wisps of dust with a fractious forepaw. The brilliant sun shone whitely upon the old Texan's face and those of the handful of men mounted behind him.

Tamblyn's rasping voice bellowed along the trail:

'You ain't seen the last of me, Conant, an' you damned nesters! I have a move up my sleeve an' I'll run Flyin' Spur beef over yore blamed corn-patches yet!'

He made a quick gesture with a mahogany coloured hand and his remaining wranglers wheeled their horses about with his and made off along the trail towards the curve around the rock shoulder.

Fourteen

As Tamblyn and his small mounted party disappeared around the shoulder of rock, Conant and Hannaway slithered down from the cover of the pine branches.

Columns of dark smoke still spiralled up from the eastern points of the ridge where the gutted remains of the Apsley and Diffin homesteads were situated. A light banner of hoof-risen dust lingered at the point where the Flying Spur riders had rounded the shoulder. Hannaway faced Conant, his lean features set grimly.

'What now?' he asked. 'Do we take after 'em?'

'No,' Conant replied, 'we'll wait and see what their next move is. The odds are evened up some now that some of Tamblyn's men have deserted him, but we won't sit around the homesteads waitin' for him. When he comes back with his remaining rannies, we won't be there.'

'What do you mean?' Hannaway wanted to know. 'What are we goin' to do with the women an' kids?'

Conant turned slightly and nodded to a rise of land,

studded with live oaks, sweeping up some distance at the rear of Hannaway's corn-patch.

'We hide ourselves up there in the live oaks an' wait to see what those Flyin' Spur devils will try to pull off,' he stated.

They made their way back to the homestead and the change of position was made, the women and children being concealed in the deep oak stands along the sunlit upsweep of the rise. Conant took his weary little bronc from the stable and Hannaway and the Diffins led their animals into the clutter of trees.

The morning lengthened towards noon without Tamblyn and his remaining gun-crew showing themselves.

Conant, the Diffin brothers and Gerry Hannaway squatted on the fringe of the oak stand, repeaters cradled in their arms, watching the small homestead buildings, huddled down the rise in the blaze of the high sun.

'What do you figure them Flyin' Spur hellions are up to?' Bill Diffin asked.

'No tellin',' Conant grunted. 'Maybe they went back to the ranch for more men, if there are any left at the Flyin' Spur.'

'I don't like it,' Seth snorted. 'That old Texas ranni-han may have lost some of his men, but he's as tough as all hell. He likely has some smart-alicky plan up his sleeve!'

The sun reached its mid-day zenith and the watchers held their positions without any move from the trail approaching the homestead. Conant, alone, moved to another position at the edge of the oak stand from where he had a clearer view of the trail which swept around the hunching shoulder of land.

He was aware of a rustle behind him and turned around to see Mildred Apsley approaching, carrying her Winchester. She sat down on the scrubby brown grass which grew between the live oaks. Conant found himself appraising the gently moulded features of the girl, brightened by the shafts of bright sunlight spearing through the gaps in the summer-profuse leaves over their heads. Looking at her, he became acutely aware once more of his own bloodstained and battle-scarred appearance.

'What do you think Tamblyn and his men will do?' she asked calmly.

'Anybody's guess,' Conant answered. 'The few he's got left don't look like anythin' special in the way of fightin' men – those with any brains had savvy enough to quit – but, at least, we ain't fightin' the odds we had against us a little time back.'

The girl remained silent, narrowing her eyes against the glare of the sun and looking down the rise to the heat-warped buildings of the Hannaway homestead. Sprawled, stiffening in the dust now, at various points on the fringe of the homestead yard, were the bodies of those Flying Spur men killed by Conant after he hustled Mildred into the homestead while those shot by the force holding the house and Hannaway and Conant from their roost in the twin pines were tumbled in limp heaps along the trail.

'Big odds,' Mildred said at length, as if half musing to herself. 'All the time I've been out here, I've realized that homesteaders are up against big odds. Not just human odds. It seems as if the very land is against you – it's cactus and rock sand and it seems to fight back when you plant corn and try to make something resembling a farm out of it!'

'Sure,' Conant agreed, 'but it's good land, for all that. It's big an' wide an' a man couldn't wish to live in a better place – if men with ideas about building cattle empires didn't have other ideas about running peaceable folk off.'

'What made Tamblyn the way he is?' she asked. 'Why is he so bitter? Why does he want this ridge – it isn't good land to run cattle on, even I know that. Why can't he leave the homesteaders here in peace?'

'I don't know,' Conant confessed. 'He didn't want the ridge until homesteaders showed upon it, first the Mormons, then the settlers of my old man's and Andy Tyzack's time and now you. I figure somethin' got into him after the war. He came to Arizona out of Texas, like a lot of Southern veterans. He got himself a section of land and started runnin' Texas longhorn cows. Maybe he figured this was his land – his kingdom, maybe – he lost everythin' in the war, but he was holdin' on to this an' determined to make things hard for anyone who settled close to it.'

'It must be something like that,' Mildred conceded. 'Most other people would be content with the section of the Spanish Saddle range Tamblyn owns.'

'Most others, maybe,' the gunfighter agreed, 'but not Tamblyn. I figure he never got over the Confederacy bein' licked an' he still wants to fight anythin' that crosses his path as a way of workin' off his spleen.'

As soon as the sentence was off his lips, Conant

stiffened, his head canted alertly in the direction of the trail sweeping toward the Hannaway holding. The thump of a single horse's hooves grew loud along the trail and a finger of sun-touched dust rose beyond the hunched shoulder pushing into the banner of the trail.

'A rider comin'!' he hissed to the Diffins and Hannaway some yards away. 'Get the women an' kids well back in the trees!'

He motioned for Mildred to move back into the shade of the oaks.

'Don't let them see the white of yore dress, we don't want them to know we're up here!'

A single horseman came loping around the shoulder of rock and sand, thundering along the trail in the direction of the homestead. A rider who sat his animal with a peculiar floppiness.

As he headed for the twin pines between which he had to pass before entering the homestead yard, his sombrero fell to the ground. A yip of realization came from Bill Diffin:

'Hey! That ain't no man, it's a dummy!'

'Yeah,' Conant responded. 'They sent a dummy rider along the trail to see if we're still in trees to snipe at 'em – or in the house to open fire from there!'

Silently, the men in the live oak stand watched the horse and its dummy rider pass between the trees, pull itself to a whinnying halt as it came close to the scent of blood from the stiffening corpses close to the homestead yard, circle and trot back towards the shoulder along the trail behind which Tamblyn's men were concealed. The dummy rider flopped grotesquely as the horse went.

'So, now they know there's no danger of getting caught in our gun-trap again – what's the next move?' Conant muttered to himself.

Secretly, he had a fear that one of the young Quillan children, being cared for by Hannaway's wife and daughter deep in the trees would begin to cry and betray their position.

The drumming tattoo of hooves came and a small knot of riders with the easily recognizable figure of Arch Tamblyn at their head swept around the shoulder and down the trail at a headlong lick for the Hannaway homestead.

'What the blazes is this move?' Gerry Hannaway queried from his concealed position as he watched the dust-raising horses thunder along the trail below.

Grimly, the watchers lying at the fringe of the oak stand watched the Flying Spur bunch pound into the homestead yard. They yanked their animals to a quick halt. Tamblyn and several of the others raised their arms in fast jerking motions. Small objects flew from them, some to land on the warped wooden roof, others to fall beside the walls and the door. Then, the Flying Spur raiders wheeled their horses about and split the wind in the direction from which they came.

Gerry Hannaway's voice breathed colourful profanity through the fringe of the oak stand on the rise.

'The stinkin' sons! That was dynamite! They threw sticks of dynamite at my home! If I get my hands on Tamblyn. . . .' His threat was lost in the bellowing of a tremendous explosion from the homestead down below. In a great gush of flame and smoke, the wooden building was thrown against the sun in a shambles of flying timbers. As the remains of the homestead were hurled into the air in the spout of flame and rubble, Conant came to his feet and ran between the trees towards the round-eyed Diffins and Hannaway.

'Come on!' he urged. 'Let's get our cayuses an' take after 'em!'

Down on the ribbon of the trail, the Flying Spur men were riding furiously back the way they came. Conant and the homesteaders reached their animals, swung speedily into their saddles, piloted their mounts through the close-bunched live oaks and went thundering down the rise, flourishing weapons and with Conant in the lead.

A haze of dust palled over the ruins of the dynamited homestead and a child was crying loudly in the live oaks. On the sun-washed trail, one of the Flying Spur riders turned, saw the four riders pounding down the rise and bellowed:

'It's Conant and the nesters!'

Up at the head of the knot of riders, the spike-moustached, wind-burned face of Arch Tamblyn turned about. The sun put a bright sheen on hastily drawn sixguns among the riding Flying Spur marauders. Conant, the Diffin brothers, and Hannaway reached the homestead yard with its freshly-settled shambles of the house and the thick haze of dust. They rowelled their animals madly to take after the Flying Spur riders, now drawing close to the shoulder of rock baulked across the trail.

Someone pegged a whining shot back at them.

Gerry Harmaway, in a white fury at the loss of his homestead, triggered a couple of ineffective shots in answer. Then, the Tamblyn bunch was whirling around the shoulder in a flurry of dry dust.

Mead Conant rode like a man possessed of a dozen devils, hacking spur rowels into horseflesh. He had shoved his Winchester into his saddle-boot now and he led the homesteaders with a drawn six-gun gripped in one hand.

This must be showdown, he knew. This was where he tripped his triggers on behalf of his father, his brothers, Apsley and the Quillans in a final fury of gunsmoke against Arch Tamblyn and the remaining men of his slick-trigger crew. He realized the danger of that shoulder of rock and sand which humped itself like a wedge into the trail. Tamblyn and his half-dozen gunnies were around it now; they could use it as cover and, if they had more dynamite, they could toss it around the shoulder full into the pursuing party of homesteaders.

'Watch out for 'em!' he bellowed at the top of his lungs. 'They've got cover—' His voice was lost in the sharp blast of a rifle. A shell zipped close to his head, a shell fired from the top of the hump of land around which the trail snaked.

Conant reared his lathered bronc back into an abrupt halt.

'Hit the dirt!' he warned. 'They're up there on the shoulder!'

There was no need for the warning. The brothers Diffin and Gerry Hannaway were already out of saddle-leather and slithering among cactus and rocks, blasting up at the shoulder with bucking guns. Another repeater shell screamed through the air and an angry flight of six-gun slugs zipped into the dry earth, gushing up spouts of dust.

Conant came off the back of his bronc to hit the ground in a slithering tumble. Slugs were snarling off the shoulder and slapping into the sun-hammered earth.

The gunfighter lay on his stomach, both Colts drawn. It was difficult to distinguish the Flying Spur men up there on the hump of land for the homesteaders were so positioned as to have the sun in their eyes.

Hannaway and the Diffins were blazing away wildly, their shots seeming to have no effect. Conant saw what appeared to be a black sombrero move among a clutter of long armed saguaro cactus on the sun-washed ochre of the hump of land. He plugged a couple of shots at it, but it ducked from sight quickly.

Shots continued to rain down from the hump of land. The homesteaders and gunfighters were spread out, each seeking what little cover the heat-split rocks and the cactus and thorn at the side of the trail offered.

Suddenly, something came whirling through the air off the shoulder of land. It hit the hot dust and then rolled with a devilishly slow motion to come to rest perhaps ten yards from where Mead Conant crouched behind scant rock cover. He saw it and regarded it with a cold, almost clinical curiosity for a moment that seemed completely detached from time.

A bundle of half-a-dozen dynamite sticks tied together with baling wire and with a dangerously short fuse spluttering red sparks at one end!

Fifteen

The long moment, detached from time, came to an end.

Conant sheathed his six-guns in his holsters and came up from behind the rock like an uncoiling spring and began to run at a crouched and headlong charge for the spluttering bundle of dynamite. As he crunched over the dry shale, shots barked and bullets whanged around him from the Flying Spur men on the shoulder. Hannaway and the Diffin brothers, realizing that Conant was full in the open now and a sitting target for Tamblyn and his gunmen, blazed up a covering crackle of fire up at the wedge of land.

Conant reached the bundle of dynamite sticks, saw how dangerously short was the burning fuse, grabbed the bundle and hurled it with all his might up at the shoulder of land. He saw it twist lazily in the air, a thin plume of smoke trailing from it, then he threw himself full length to the ground, snatching his guns from their holsters as he went.

Sprawling in the hot dust, he felt the ground rumble under him and saw earth, rock and sand gushing upwards from the side of the hump of land in a

147

red-centred splash of flame. An agonized yell sounded, mingled with the roar of the explosion.

Conant came to his feet again and began to hare for the trail where the horses of his party jumped in fright, threatening to bolt. He waved for the others to follow, flourishing a six-gun in the air.

'Come on!' he cried hoarsely. 'Get around the shoulder quick!'

The Diffins and Hannaway came out of cover and ran in his wake with all the speed they could muster.

They caught their panicky horses and were quickly asaddle, riding like the wind at Conant's back.

They rounded the shoulder with hooves pounding under them. At the rear of the hump, Tamblyn was coming down its slope with only four men following him, one of them clutching an injured arm. The Flying Spur owner and his companions were making for the group of fractious horses they had tethered at the foot of the hump where a fringe of saguaro stood with widespread arms.

The injured man stumbled and fell to the ground, slithering down the dry shale with a squawk and finally lying still. Tamblyn and the three gunhands with him reached their horses and mounted up as Conant and his companions came splitting the wind along the trail.

A wildly aimed slug sang through the air as Tamblyn turned in his saddle, triggering his six-gun into flashing life. Then, he put spurs to the animal and took off along the trail a few yards ahead of the gunfighter and the homesteaders, he and his companions spur-raking their mounts with legs working like pistons.

Conant was riding to the fore of his party, gripping his saddle with his knees and holding a Peacemaker in each hand. He blazed purposely ill-aimed shots after the fleeing Tamblyn and his riders.

Through the swirling hoof-risen dust, he bellowed:

'Tamblyn, stop! Stop, or take it in the back!'

Still, Tamblyn and his riders hurtled along the trail in headlong panic. Conant levelled a six-gun, drew a bead on one of the rear legs of the rancher's mount and fired. The slug took the animal at the rear of the knee, sending it into a whirling tumble. Tamblyn was pitched from the saddle as the animal slithered down. He hit the ground with his head shielded by a crooked arm, a reflex action to which a hundred round-up and trail-herd tosses had conditioned him. The rancher rolled along the ground ultimately to stop in a head-long sprawl. His three companions, without looking back, continued to hoof it at top speed along the trail.

'We'll take after 'em!' shouted Gerry Hannaway.

'No, let them ride to blazes,' Conant answered. 'They're only cheap border scum – we've got the big fish netted!'

He took his bronc forward towards the sprawling form of Tamblyn and yanked it to a halt, training his guns on the rancher.

'Don't try grabbin' for yore iron,' Conant warned, noting the fallen man's six-gun lying a few yards from him. 'We got you dead to rights, Tamblyn!'

Tamblyn, winded and wheezing, felt that cold quail of fear twist in his stomach. Looking at the sun-sheened twin guns in the hands of the lean, sun-browned man who faced him from the saddle of the snorting bronc, he realized that he was indeed an old man.

'All right, Conant,' he gasped wearily. 'You win! Give me a hand up!'

Mead Conant said: 'You're through, Tamblyn, you an' the Flyin' Spur! You'll never run cows over North Ridge; in fact you'll never run cows anywhere on the Spanish Saddle range again. You're puttin' yore outfit up for sale an' you'll repay these homesteaders for what you did to their homes.'

Arch Tamblyn, divested of his gun-gear and leaning against one of the saguaro cactus, glowered at the gunfighter at whose back stood the Diffins and Gerry Hannaway.

'What d'you mean, Conant?' he grated. 'You ain't got that kind of say-so—'

'I'm givin' you yore skin, Tamblyn,' Conant cut in. 'It's either this or hang under Federal law. For what you an' yore gunnies did on North Ridge, I should smoke you down like a mad dog, but I'm givin' you yore skin. You're an old man, Tamblyn. Someday, you might start gettin' a conscience an' I'd sooner leave you to try to live with it than push a slug in you. You might start gettin' to think about my father an' brothers an' that Quillan couple an' young Apsley up on North Ridge. I'm givin' you a choice: you either sell out an' clear plumb out of Arizona or I take you to the nearest United States marshal. There is no law around here of any kind since Tyzack was killed, but there's a marshal in Tombstone. You can take yore choice. Which is it to be?'

With the bleak eyes of Conant and the hard gaze of the homesteaders fixed on him, Arch Tamblyn studied the ground. There was a sag to his shoulders and the wind and sun-burned mask of his face had become grey and aged visibly. He made a gesture of absolute futility.

'All right, Conant. I'll sell up an' clear out. Like you say, I'm an old man.'

'Who's yore lawyer?'

'Eli Frick, in Huajillo.'

'Climb into yore saddle, we're ridin' to see him. You Diffin boys better come along as witnesses to this deal. Gerry, you go back up the ridge an' settle the women an' the youngsters down. The Quillan homestead is the only place left standin', you better move 'em all in there for the time bein'.'

The homesteaders nodded and Hannaway turned his horse for North Ridge, while the brothers Diffin swung into their saddles to ride close behind Mead Conant as he escorted Tamblyn into the township of Huajillo.

They rode out of the ridge country, crossed the Spanish Saddle rangeland with its grama grass belly-high to the horses and came into the sunbaked little cowtown as a slow-riding procession.

Groups of loafers standing under the peeled and warped awnings of the broadwalks watched the spectacle of a dejected, gunless, Arch Tamblyn being escorted into town. Some of them shook off their indolence and ambled across the street when they saw the party dismount outside Eli Frick's office.

News that Tamblyn was making gunsmoke against

the North Ridge nesters had held Huajillo in its grip since the previous day and this, it seemed, was something worthy of their attention – the owner of the Spanish Saddle range and this town being escorted in by a gunslinger and two nesters.

Conant prodded the rancher into the low adobe building which housed Eli Frick's legal office.

Frick was a small man with steel-rimmed spectacles and a frock-coat of rusty black. He was sitting behind a roll-top desk, littered with papers, doing nothing more important than dozing when the party came in. His watery eyes opened suddenly at the arrival of Tamblyn and his escort, fixing the four with a querying gaze.

'Mr Tamblyn is sellin' out his outfit,' Conant said sharply. 'He wants you to draw up the papers an' put the Flyin' Spur up for sale. You handle the whole business, Mr Tamblyn won't be around this country much longer.'

Frick's eyes opened ever wider behind the lenses of his spectacles.

'Is this true?' he asked in a voice whose wheezy edge spoke of a long acquaintance with the bottle.

'It's true,' growled Arch Tamblyn. 'I'm sellin' the Flyin' Spur an' movin' out.'

'Where are the title deeds and all the other papers?' Eli Frick wanted to know.

'Back in my safe at the Flyin' Spur,' the rancher replied.

'Then we'll have to ride over there and draw up the papers,' the lawyer said. He stood up and moved across the small and dusty office, giving the gun-hung

Conant a wide berth as he passed him.

'Okay,' agreed Conant. 'We'll ride to the Flyin' Spur an' these two men will witness the arrangements,' he added with a nod to the Diffin brothers.

Sixteen

At the Flying Spur, deserted save for the Mexican servant and the ancient Chinese cook, Tamblyn led the way into his living room with its fieldstone fireplace over which hung various weapons and grand trophies such as a mountain-lion's head; the huge iron-bound safe stood close by, near to the window and the cabinet which housed the bottle of good liquor. With Conant, the Diffins and Eli Frick at his back, the rancher produced a key from a pocket and opened the safe. He took a bundle of papers from it and handed them to the lawyer. Frick studied them with his nose close to the paper.

'This property of yours is worth a large amount of money,' Frick observed slowly.

'You think I don't know that?' snapped Tamblyn. 'Draw up the paper an' let's get it over with.'

'The paper?' queried Frick. 'There's no paper to be drawn up other than an inventory to be taken so I can put a detailed account of the ranch's value on the market.'

'There is a paper to be drawn up, Frick,' Conant told him slowly. 'One agreeing that he gives fifty per cent of whatever the Flyin' Spur brings to be divided among the North Ridge homesteaders.'

Frick goggled nervously at the tall, gun-heavy man.

'Is that what you wish, Mr Tamblyn?' he asked, his eyes squinting over the steel tops of his eye-glasses.

'Yeah, you blamed old fool,' snarled the old Texan. 'Get the paper drawn up *pronto!*'

From the inner regions of his rusty frock-coat, Eli Frick produced a sheet of legal paper, requested a pen, sat down at the table and began to write a long document couched in legal terms. Conant, Tamblyn and the Diffins read it over. Tamblyn duly signed it and the Diffin brothers added their signatures as witnesses.

Tamblyn, wearily, crossed to the cabinet between the window and the fieldstone fireplace and opened it to produce the bottle of whiskey and a couple of glasses.

'You're a plumb shrewd *hombre*, Conant,' he praised grudgingly. 'You got me dead to rights, for sure. Took my place from me all legal.'

'You get yore neck an' a fifty per cent cut of the price the place brings, which is more than you deserve by a considerable damnsight.'

Tamblyn grinned a hard grin. He poured two glasses of neat whiskey.

'You're a hell of a feller, Conant,' he commented. 'Yore old man was a Rebel, wasn't he?'

'Yeah, he was a Rebel, same as you – but that didn't stop you turnin' yore gunnies loose on him twelve years ago.'

Tamblyn ignored the observation. He regarded Conant, still holding the whiskey bottle in his hand.

'You're a fit son for a Rebel, Conant,' he said slowly. 'Too bad you see things in a plumb peculiar fashion. You an' me might have done big things if you'd been cast in another mould. Have a drink with me, just to show there's no hard feelin's?'

Conant shook his head.

'I wouldn't drink with you if I was chokin' with thirst, Tamblyn – an' there are hard feelings!' he retorted.

The old Texan pulled a wry face.

'Have it yore way,' he drawled, 'but I'll have a drink.'

Conant took his eyes from the rancher for a brief instant, then he was suddenly aware of Tamblyn's arm looping forward and the heavy whiskey bottle hurtled through the air to crash against the side of his temple. Conant almost lost his balance as a stunning shock jarred through his head. He staggered to one side, heard Seth Diffin yell a sharp warning and Eli Frick squawk.

Then, his eyes focused and he saw Tamblyn making a grab for a Remington, mounted above the head of the mountain lion over the fireplace.

Even as he grabbed for his own guns, his head still reeling with the shock of the blow from the bottle, he saw Tamblyn swing the barrel of the Remington on him, his dark eyes in the wrinkled mask of a face glittering.

'This is loaded, Conant, an' I'm goin' to give you all hell!' grated Tamblyn. There was a sudden flurry of activity as the Diffins and Frick, at Conant's back, jumped out of range.

The Remington in Tamblyn's hand barked out a slamming blast.

Even as it did so, Mead Conant ducked low, feeling the hot belch of the weapon searing the air over his head. The twin Peacemakers looped up out of his holsters and levelled on Tamblyn. Just as the rancher, his face twisted into a grimace of hatred, was about to fire again, one of Conant's guns slammed. Arch Tamblyn tottered back through a sea of gunsmoke, hitting the wall and finally slumping to the floor with a heavy thud.

Eli Frick came up from behind the chair where he had taken shelter, moving slowly, like a turtle coming out of its shell.

'He's dead,' said Bill Diffin without emotion.

'Yeah,' breathed his lanky brother, bending to retrieve the unbroken bottle of whiskey from the floor. 'Let's have a drink!'

Conant rode alongside the Diffins, mounting North Ridge. He rode with a vision, hardly noticing the nester brothers at his side.

In that last slam of guns at the Flying Spur, it seemed, the grudges he held on behalf of his father, Clay, Lloyd, the Quillans and Dave Apsley had passed out of him. Gone, too, was the haunting notion that his whole life was nothing but a progression towards a boot-hill grave with a sardonic epitaph. There was something more to it, now. He would throw his lot in with the North Ridge nesters, help them to rebuild their homes and make something worthwhile out of the land.

Mildred was much in his thoughts. He thought of her as she was those few days before, gentle, horrified at his action at the Flying Spur; he thought of her after the killing of her brother, noticeably hardened and wielding a Winchester. He hadn't liked that. It was the beginning of a bitterness that might change her whole personality. He liked her best as the gentle nester girl who bestowed shy glances on him that first night of his stay at the Apsley homestead.

They rode steadily, each concerned with his own thoughts. They reached the sweep of the ridge-top trail and rode it until they came through the aspens and the live-oaks to the Quillan homestead.

Hannaway, his wife and sons and daughter, came out of the house to greet them.

And Mildred.

She came slowly, smiling, from the house. Conant saw at once that here was the nester girl of his first evening on North Ridge, and he saw, more clearly than ever before, that he was her kind of man – a nester.

He came out of the saddle, dusty, scarred, blood-crusted and weary, and Mildred came forward eagerly. They looked at each other only for an instant, then he took her in his arms and kissed her, in front of the whole goggling bunch of them.

Mildred nestled up to him. He could smell the fragrance of her spun-gold hair.

He was a man walking away from boot-hill.